I0582097

CROWN OF BROKEN PROMISES

AN EMPIRE OF CURSES AND DREAMS PREQUEL

THE NIGHT AND RAIN SERIES

SUSAN PERSON

Copyright © 2025 by Susan Person

ISBN **978-1-953412-28-7**

All rights reserved.

No part of this book may be reproduced in any form or by any electronic or mechanical means, including information storage and retrieval systems, without written permission from the author, except for the use of brief quotations in a book review. No part of this book may be used for AI purposes without express written permission from the author.

Cover design by Laura at Spellbinding Design.

For all those who would choose the unicorn horn

AUTHOR'S NOTE

Dear Reader - Please be advised that this book series contains content that may be upsetting for some readers. Should you wish to learn more information for your best reading experience, please scan the QR code below for additional details and content notes.

CONTENTS

CROWN OF BROKEN PROMISES

PART ONE

TRAITOR

Letter in the War Museum

From an undated private letter written by General Daphina to King Veran held in the War Museum. The curators assume this was sent in the weeks leading up to General Daphina's great sacrifice. The gift she references is still a mystery to this day and many assume it is hidden in the palace. Or perhaps only those with certain magic can locate it as many of our powers are ancestral.

> *My dearest King,*
> *We have managed to push the enemy back,*
> *but they seem to know our every move. I must*
> *concede that I believe a traitor is among us, and a*

powerful one. Plans that were only known by a few until the day of our advancement were anticipated all too precisely. I fear our royal correspondence may have been compromised or intercepted. I'm sending my most trusted soldier, who can vanyshen to you, to share the details. Please grant him an audience. I pray to our Goddess Nyx and the goddesses and gods with her to protect you.

I hope you are keeping the gift I gave you close as a reminder of my commitment to you. It will strengthen your wind magic to an impenetrable field. We will triumph.

Forever and faithfully yours,
General Daphina

CHAPTER I

THE PATH

GEMMA

Mother's stories haunted me as I laid the wreath of moonflowers at the edge of the forest with the white stone wall of the palace at my back. The subtle sweetness of the blooms meandered on the light breeze. Arianna had prepared the floral arrangement because even though the damn flowers were only supposed to bloom at night, they bloomed on command for her. My sister and Mother both loved them, and Ari's massive garden Mother had cultivated with her was proof of it. Mother left us ten years ago, and my unhealed heart ached for the loss. Grief ravaged me on a regular basis and were it not for my sworn protector, Cyrus, thoughts of how weak Mother had been at the end and my helplessness would have consumed me. How sallow her coloring was. How gray her dark hair had turned. How she had told me goodbye and asked me to send my sister in. Then, the next time I saw her, Mother was gone. Goddesses and gods, I hoped she found peace now.

Her magic waned as her body weakened, and in delirium she'd woven together stories of the war she'd told only to me. The tales she shared I'd never heard until then, and I still didn't know if they were true—if they even could be. Every day, the chronicles nagged at me in the recesses of my mind as if they wanted me to remember events that weren't mine. Mother told me of a thriving city with lots of people and described a thing called technology. Powered by something other than our magic, it allowed for strange devices used to communicate and coaches that didn't need horses. I thought it was madness, but she seemed lucid at the time.

She told me to remember her in the forest, so each year on her death day, I came out to the edge of the forbidden woods and let my grief unleash itself. Wind swirled around me wafting in the soft scents of the foliage as if my affinity sought to wrap me up in a protective cocoon. My sister, Arianna, was only ten when Mother passed. I thought Ari might start coming out with me this year, but when I asked her, she broke down in sobs, locking herself in her room. Val, her best friend, was the only person she'd let in. She wasn't ready to face the pain, and I understood. We all handled grief in our own way.

Branches cracked nearby in the thicket. The woodland wasn't called the Forbidden Forest as a child's tale. Souls imprisoned by dark magic were trapped during the war. I stumbled backward over a stone, expecting Cyrus to be there. He wasn't. I reached down that strong bond that only a fae and a unicorn who'd been bonded could experience. *Cyrus. Something is in the forest.*

Why are you there?

I'd slipped away and blocked the bond to be alone. He didn't like me coming near the forest. I usually couldn't keep him out of my head for long, so I was surprised he hadn't found me already. Nothing was after me though. I was fine. *Never mind.*

I'm already on my way.

I heard his hooves beat the ground and relaxed, knowing he was close. The sound of four steps pounding the dirt changed to footfalls as he drew closer.

"I told you this was a bad idea," he said, his tone a biting hiss. He'd been more and more cross with me lately. Not that he was more than cordial with anyone, but I'd thought as my bonded he'd be more friendly with me.

"As I tell you every year, it was my mother's dying request to be remembered. I don't understand it, but I will honor her."

Branches broke a little farther away. My muscles tightened, preparing to fight. "I thought there was no fauna living in the forest. Only flora."

"There shouldn't be," he whispered.

An agonizing groan reached my ears. The fight left me. Someone, possibly a subject of my kingdom, was hurt, and leaving them injured in the dreadful forest wasn't an option I entertained. I took a couple of steps, my gaze at the ground beyond the edge of the forest line for the first time. The damp earth scent blended with the decay of leaves, but there was something else. It smelled more like life here—not overpowering death as I expected.

"Don't, Gemma. Stop." Cyrus's deep voice rose with

each word, but I ignored him, treading forward. Then, he was in my head. *Don't go any farther. It will not end well.*

"Fuck," a male voice shouted. I froze, closer to the man than I realized based on how much louder he sounded.

"Gemma." Cyrus drew my name out in a huff like he had when I was a child. "This is reckless. We can send scouts."

"He might need help," I said. My guardian wouldn't normally leave an injured person.

"It's the dead trapped in this forsaken place," Cyrus said. "They trick those who enter and stray from the single path in and out."

"Path?" I turned to face him. No one had ever mentioned a safe path before. Not once in my life had I heard of it. Cyrus was in his unicorn form, directly opposite in coloring to his twin brother, who'd claimed my sister as his charge. I should be flattered he needed to be in his natural state to keep up with me, but his fae persona carved out a prohibited place of honor in my imagination.

"I shouldn't have told you, but I will tell you if you leave this place with me now."

"Better yet, show me the path." I scouted the area but didn't see any sign of where someone might have traversed the terrain. Everything looked overgrown like it hadn't been entered in years.

"No," he said, his voice firm. "That is a terrible idea."

"Fine." I started forward, scouring the ground for anything that looked like a path that had been traveled. "I'll just explore the forest on my own."

"You are insufferable." He stomped up next to me. "You're going the wrong way."

"Then show me." I held my hands out at my sides. He could say no, and I'd probably follow him home. I suspected he wouldn't, though, because he stood still.

Cyrus blew out a huff that steamed in the cool air of the forest. "You stay beside me at all times."

"Whatever you say, big guy." I teased him to deal with my nerves. As excited as I was to explore a new area, the injured man took precedence. Despite how terrified the woods made me, my father had told me my entire life to not let fear stop me, and I'd lived by that—more so since Mother passed. Except when it came to the Forgotten Forest...Father had prohibited entry into the woodland long before my birth—at a time when, according to our historians, the land was still barren from the Great War. Mother rarely spoke on the subject as if there was a version of the truth she wouldn't or couldn't divulge.

"Must you always call me old? I'm still young and vibrant for a unicorn."

I patted his shoulder. "I know you are."

Cyrus looked from my hand to my gaze, an annoyed expression on his face. He herded me over to a path, overgrown from lack of use. I was shocked it was really there and even more so that someone would venture into the area. A few paver stones jutted up in random positions, long forgotten like the forest. I stared out into the dense wood and wondered if apparitions truly wandered the expanse or if those had been stories told to keep us clear. Cyrus and I had been in the area for at least an hour and hadn't seen anything. I started to wonder whether the man's voice I heard was indeed someone who was injured or a trapped phantom.

Cyrus stopped. "We should turn back."

"Why?" I paused next to him. He couldn't be tired. His stamina outpaced mine in training every time. I saw nothing in front of us but forest. It'd been some time since we heard the man's voice. The only sounds were the breeze rustling the leaves and our breathing. "I want to see it to the end. How much farther is it?"

"We're close, but we will not be alone there."

"Our enemy?" I lowered my voice to a whisper. Adrenaline spiked in my veins, making me jittery, but I readied myself.

"Possibly," he said. "Likely." He didn't seem that concerned and certainly not afraid.

If he wasn't that worried, then I didn't see a need to be either. Two hundred years had passed with very little interaction. Father had mentioned a few skirmishes but nothing to threaten our borders in a significant way. What if they wanted to mend the kingdoms? "Perhaps this is an opportunity to renew relations with them. Maybe even incorporate them into our kingdom if they are as desolate from the war as we believe."

Surely, two centuries after losing the war to our kingdom broke their ties to the dark fae ways I'd learned about with the historians. Time changed us all, and this kingdom wouldn't be an exception. Would it? And if they had evolved to be better people, our kingdoms would both benefit from trade—theirs more than ours since their defeat left them on the verge of collapse. It seemed fitting that, as the next generation, my destiny brought me the chance to heal the connection between our two lands.

"I don't think it's a good idea to engage, Gemma." He blocked the path with his body. "They are not like us. There are many differences."

"Yes, yes. Father talks about how darkness rules them and the terrible magic they practice. But Nyx is one of our goddesses, and she is darkness itself. She's not bad, so that doesn't mean they are inherently bad."

"What you say is true, of course." He jerked his head toward the path.

I peered around him to see an elf dressed in clothing of shapes and patterns I'd never seen in our kingdom. He had a shirt with no collar on it, like a man's undershirt but thicker, and a brown jacket over it with four pockets. He wore similar color pants with a large pocket on each thigh. My gaze traveled from his curly, blondish-brown hair and snagged on his soulful amber eyes. His mouth gaped open as he looked at Cyrus and then me. The handsome man's full lips curved into a smile.

My own mouth returned the casual gesture without my bidding. I couldn't believe this meeting was real. A soft aura glowed around the stranger, different from any others I'd seen. My ability to see auras had manifested just before Mother's death, and Cyrus was the only one who knew I saw them. He'd trained me on how to shield myself when in large groups. We'd practiced so much that it was second nature for me to put it up when around lots of people. Large assemblies overwhelmed me with emanations because I wanted to understand them. It left me weakened. Smaller groups seldom strained me, and at least with those or in one-on-one circumstances, drawing back was easier.

Ari's aura radiated a dark purple mixed with moonlight and traces of red. Although I only glimpsed it one time, Mother's had been white, bright like the sun. She was the only one I saw with one color. Father's was hidden or suppressed. I never could see his. But this man's was warm and inviting like a morning embraced by the most beautiful sunrise.

"Hello," he said, his accent slightly different from ours. I knew for certain at that moment he was from the kingdom on the other side, but nothing about him frightened me. None of my internal alarms warned against him.

"Good morning," I replied, inclining my head.

"What business do you have here?" Cyrus asked, his tone brisk.

I cut my gaze to him. He'd been short with me and others but never so rude.

"I'm out looking for some medicinal plants." The man patted a bag on his side. "My name is Laurel."

He came forward with his hand extended. I took it in mine, and he bowed. His aura circled my hand like a gentle caress and brushed inside my chest. Intriguing. I'd never experienced anything like it.

"Gemma," I said. "It's a pleasure."

"What a beautiful name." His tone was warm and inviting.

I inclined my head toward him in thanks. "Were you

calling for help earlier? I...we heard someone in need and came to assist."

"No, but the forest is full of spirits who cannot escape. What you heard was probably one of them. They like to play games with the living who acknowledge them. Harmless in most cases."

Most cases... I touched my throat. Were there other cases when people disappeared and didn't come back?

Laurel held out an arm, turning in the opposite direction of my kingdom. "May I escort you back?"

My nerves kicked in, and I clasped my hands in front of me to hide the shaking. We couldn't go further with this man, but I desperately wanted to. I wanted to know more about him and what herbs he risked a run-in with the ghosts haunting the forest. "We can find our way. You have herbs to collect."

"I'd just finished when you happened upon me." He smiled and left his arm out.

I glanced back at Cyrus. He gave a shake of his head. *No, Gemma. This is not only a bad idea but risks death.*

If I refused him now, he'd see us go in a different direction and figure out Cyrus and I belonged in the other kingdom. That would certainly lead to death, ours or his. *He'll suspect us if we don't. We can walk a little way and then figure out an excuse.*

"Very well." I slipped my arm in his.

CHAPTER 2

No Wall

Laurel had been the epitome of politeness in conversation and poise. He took my hand and helped me over a fallen tree. The bark was slippery from the dampness of the forest, but I think he just wanted to hold my hand. I didn't miss the look on his face when the contact caused a little charge between us. My heart had sped up, and I tamped it down. I could have used my wind magic to move the log, but then, I would have missed his curious expression. As we neared the edge of the forest, I saw no wall on the other side like ours. This kingdom was supposed to have a much larger barrier made of unicorn horns, but there was nothing there. I cut my eyes side to side, thoroughly confused by what didn't stand on this side of the forest.

Cyrus, did you know there was no wall here?

Yes. His thought came through our bond so curtly I winced.

"Miss Gemma, I would very much like to see to it that

you eat after our trek through the forest. Would you join me for a late breakfast?"

Noises I'd never heard before crowded in around us. Squeaks and whirls and roars like mild thunder were in the distance, but there were other sounds...voices...so many voices. I wanted to cover my ears against the cacophony, but I wanted to take them all in too. Glimpses of buildings larger than anything I'd seen before emerged where the cobblestones circling the perimeter turned into a smooth, dark substance.

My heart wanted more—more sights of this city, more unusual dinging and clanging, and more faces to match to voices. My head tempered my eagerness, reminding me it was a bad idea. All of the newness belonged to the enemy, and I stood by the opposition. If I stayed longer, he'd figure out I wasn't a fellow citizen, and that could mean war between our kingdoms. "I'm afraid we must be going, but I enjoyed our talk."

His face softened into an almost apologetic look. He pulled a device out of his pocket and punched on the buttons. "I apologize for this. I would have preferred this not to be the way."

Guardsmen in blue and black uniforms filed out of a gate. *Fucking goddesses and gods.* I scrambled to run toward the woods, but some of them appeared out of nowhere in front of me and Cyrus. My bonded moved close to me. I glanced to the right and left, but the soldiers encircled us.

I reached for the wind. If I acted fast, I could knock them back without hurting them and give Cyrus and me a chance to run.

Don't, Cyrus said in my head. *We'll figure another way out. Don't show them your power. They could figure out you are the crown princess.*

His advice made sense. Giving away my status could give them leverage over Father. I'd have to find another way to get away. I let the wind go, and it whisked away into nothing. *How do we know they don't already know who I am?*

We don't, but we are outnumbered and have no concept of what power they have.

Laurel held his arm out as he had in the forest. I narrowed my eyes at him and refused to take his offered elbow.

"Lead the way," I said. He'd seemed so nice, but that would have been too good to be true. A nice person wouldn't have taken me and my bonded captive. Nice he was not. I'd enjoy breaking a few of his bones when I was free.

He inclined his head and guided us through the large metal gate into a courtyard. Sunlight glinted off white stones and marble stepping stones. The walkway led through an archway where another guard stood. He bowed his head toward Laurel. I'd suspected he was noble, and the building was a palace, larger than my castle and covered in white stone. My enemy's home.

Flower beds filled with shrubs and blossoms lined the wall. A black and white Iris I'd never seen before caught my eye. Next to it was a similar one with black and white stripes but a yellow center. Their beauty alternated between the beds.

Zebra irises. Cyrus sent down our bond, sounding calm but annoyed.

Zebra? That's a strange name.

It's a black and white striped animal similar to a horse, but smaller. They live in the human lands. He sounded amused, and his demeanor made me wonder if he'd lost his sanity.

That sounds...unusual. While our animals had many colors here, I'd never seen one, especially a tiny horse, with black and white stripes like the flowers.

A soft laugh came down our bond. He wasn't tense about our predicament. Maybe I'd finally driven him over the edge with my antics.

Why are you not afraid? No answer came, but heat spread over my chest. I flicked my gaze toward Laurel to find him watching me and Cyrus.

An understated doorway came into view, clearly meant to be a discreet entrance. The dark wooden frame was carved with ruins in an ancient language, but other than that, it was unassuming. More guards, dressed in light blue uniforms with silver thread, bowed. One sentry opened the door, standing at attention as we passed.

Strange lights that didn't have a flame, like our lamps, lit the way. Despite the size of the palace, it had a warm feel as if it was alive—a living, breathing community.

Laurel's fingers grasped my elbow in a tender touch. I looked where his skin met mine. My gaze slid up over his shoulders until it landed on his eyes. There was a soft, almost apologetic, set to his fine face. I hesitated. He was my enemy, but his touch was like the caress of a gentle wind. I slid my arm free, and he didn't stop me.

Warmth heated my back, and I glanced over my shoulder to see Cyrus towering over me in his human form. His golden-brown skin and dark hair both shimmered, even in the unusual light of the palace. His striking eyes and well-defined jaw were nothing less than harmonious. Although he and Marius were twins and did favor, Cyrus was the better-looking of the two. Thankfully, my bonded chose to wear a shirt when he glamoured this time. He could hold the form longer and more naturally than others, his unique gift. My core heated, and it shouldn't. *Goddesses and gods, Gemma. You're in the house of your enemy with your guardian, idiot. Control your effing self.*

Laurel led us into a large dining hall, bigger than anything in my kingdom. Pots and pans banged together beyond a door that had to lead to the kitchen. He gestured to a smaller table at the front and pulled the chair back for me. One of his men disappeared behind the door as I sat down.

He took the seat next to me, looking far too pleased with himself. "I know this must seem very awkward."

"I'm not sure what you mean." I shifted on my seat, no doubt giving away my nervousness. Cyrus took the seat next to me in his human form.

"To be in a strange kingdom with unfamiliar things must make you feel very vulnerable."

Fucking goddesses and gods. He knows, Cyrus.

Stay calm, Gemma.

I fucked up, Cyrus. His heat penetrated my skin from the close distance, but I didn't dare look at him. He'd trained me better than that.

We will get out of here. I'm already searching.

A dark-haired woman and a young man brought out several dishes of food. I didn't recognize anything except the roasted meat and root vegetables and berries. The food looked edible, and the aroma invited me to taste it. I'd need strength for the escape, but I wasn't starved for a meal.

Laurel popped a berry in his mouth, and the woman smiled at him.

"It takes more than being in the presence of a handsome man to make me feel uncomfortable," I said, reaching for a raspberry.

Laurel coughed, and the woman covered her mouth, turning toward the kitchen. She ushered the young man through the door with her.

A dark-headed man patted Laurel hard on the back. He'd appeared as if he'd stepped out of the shadows. His inky blue eyes danced with amusement. "Are you choked?"

Laurel shook his head. The two men favored each other. Cousins maybe.

"Brother, I heard we had guests." Brothers then. They didn't look that closely related. The man, who had a chiseled face like a statue, extended his hand to me. I took it, and he gave it a firm shake. "It's a pleasure to meet you. My brother doesn't usually bring such beautiful women home. I'm Rainier."

"Gemma," I replied, breaking the contact quickly. I stifled a snicker. Rainier, the same name as my friend in Agonburg. Only this Rainier was more handsome, but what I noticed most was how his aura appeared to be the twin to Ari's. That wasn't possible though. No two fae auras were the same.

Laurel's face turned a bright shade of red. "Why are you here, Rain? Don't you have a tornado to spin?"

What an odd thing to say. Rainier's face went cold at that comment—a hint at his magic abilities maybe. If Laurel was the warm wind on a bright sunny day, Rainier was the opposite—a cold rain on the darkest night. His expression went neutral.

"I'll leave you and your guest to it then, Brother." The vitriol Rainier put in those words was pure acid.

I don't like him. I shot my comment to Cyrus. Ari and I would never act that way to each other, and the hateful treatment reminded me of the stories I'd been told of this corrupt kingdom. Rainier exited as quickly as he'd entered, and I studied Laurel. He didn't look hurt but more concerned as he watched his brother leave. Laurel worried about his brother just as I did for Ari. Could it be one brother was good and one not?

There's more at play here than you've noticed. Cyrus said. *I think he has a lot on his shoulders, Gemma. That was Prince Rainier. The ruler of this kingdom.*

I cut my gaze at Cyrus, and everything seemed to slow down. *Are you sure?*

We are in the palace of the seat of this kingdom, and he is the one who wears the crown.

"You're a prince?" I blurted out to Laurel before I could think.

He winced. "Something like that. Sorry. I'm used to people just knowing."

Of course he was because he didn't interact with people from my kingdom nor I his.

"And you know who I am?" I asked, my voice hardly a whisper.

"Yes." He didn't hide it, and I wasn't sure his brother would have been as direct. Perhaps they weren't as evil in this empire as I was led to believe. Rainier's attitude ricocheted so fast that he alarmed me. Even after he left, his anger remained palpable in the room. Laurel electrified the space in a different way. I didn't trust him any more than Rainier, but Laurel's softness stirred interest in me. For that reason, I didn't use my wind magic on him.

"What do you plan to do with me?" I tucked my hands into my lap to hide them from shaking.

"If you will permit me, I'd like to educate you on the ways of this kingdom."

It wasn't a question, but he'd still phrased it in a way as to seek my consent. It was an act that showed some integrity even if he'd basically kidnapped me.

Laurel's face looked expectantly at me as if he waited for me. He blushed under my steady gaze, and a spot in the center of my chest warmed.

I nodded. He wanted to teach me about the things Mother told of in her stories, and I was fascinated by the opportunity to learn more about my mother's life. "I'd very much like to learn more about your kingdom." Particularly those strange noises I'd heard earlier, but I'd ask about those later.

"Good. Whenever you are finished eating, we'll start here today. Then, if you are up for it, we'll venture out into the city tomorrow."

I shot a quick glance at Cyrus. His eyes narrowed, but he didn't communicate through our bond. Ari and Drew, my little brother, would be fine for one night. After his mother lost her internal battle and took her own life, I cared for him as I had my sister after our mother died. He had plenty of others to take care of him, so I wasn't worried about his well-being for one night Ari was used to me disappearing at times when I went out. My outings were known among the staff, so that meant it would be at least a day before anyone would look for me. Ari started to ask me if I was going out to meet boys. When I finally gave her an answer, I'd corrected her to men. My sister was probably in her garden. That's where she'd spent every anniversary of our mother's death. The next day, every flower would bloom as if she'd infused all her grief into something good. What would Ari think if she knew I was sitting at the table with a prince of the enemy kingdom? I pushed the plate away from me. The opportunity to escape might reveal itself on his tour. "I'm ready."

CHAPTER 3
THE PIANO
GEMMA

The differences between the palace of the enemy kingdom and my castle were vast. It took hours to tour Laurel's home, and there were so many strange things he explained—electricity, phones attached to the wall, pocket-sized phones, and a room with computers that could see around the palace and talk to other parts of the kingdom. My fascination grew with each new piece of technology he introduced—the stories my mother told me confirmed. Cyrus checked in on our bond several times and assured me he was fine. Given he wouldn't leave me in danger, I relaxed a bit. He'd met up with unicorns for unicorn business. His response annoyed me, but I didn't feel unsafe here either. Still, I wondered why Laurel bothered sharing the secrets of his people. What did he have to gain by showing me these things?

We reached the end of a particularly long hallway, and he paused in front of a set of two large double doors. "I heard you are gifted in the area of music." He swung the doors open, and there were more instruments in the space than my brain could register—some I'd never seen before. A comforting aroma of wood and lacquer wafted around me. It reminded me of home, and how much I missed my siblings. A longing formed in my chest and lodged at the base of my throat. My resolve to escape was bolstered by the recollection of them sitting in our music room doing crafts while I played.

Despite the long day of crossing the forest on foot and then touring the vastness of the castle, my energy returned being near so many musical devices. Centered in the room, a beautiful grand piano stole my attention. Nothing brought me more peace after Mother passed than playing. A nudge urged me toward the instrument as if my mother coaxed me to play in her homeland. Peace was the goal here, too, so maybe some music could help us get there. "May I?"

"If you're not too tired from the day, of course."

"I'm never too tired for a piano." I glided down on the bench and ran my fingers from one end of the keyboard to the other. *Perfectly tuned.* I positioned my hands in an arch on the keyboard and tapped the notes of a sonata my mother had taught me before her death. My chest warmed at the memory as I recalled the warm sunny day. The notes blended together and danced around the room in undeniably incredible acoustics. I gave myself over to the sound and closed my eyes, seeing the beauty of each musical bar as it passed by. My magic hummed in my veins as it did every time I played this piece—like my wind magic could carry the music to my mother. I reached the end of the piece and let my eyes drift open. My grief relented for the first time in years. I exhaled, letting the weight go. It was like Mother intended it to be this way...here...with this prince. I studied him, not sure what to expect, but his facial features softened.

Laurel leaned against the piano. He reached out, his thumb brushing across my cheek, and I realized it was damp. I hadn't cried in a long time when I played that piece. He dropped his hand, and my skin chilled without his touch.

He cleared his throat. "Your talent is mesmerizing. It's like you are the music when you play."

"Thank you." My cheeks heated. "I don't usually get so emotional when I play. I guess today has been...a lot." Laurel's kingdom thrived, and I didn't know how to reconcile that with what I'd been told by my father and the historians. I observed nothing warped by evil or coated in dark magic. Laurel's aura embodied light. Why had he forced me into his palace then?

"I can understand why that would be. You are probably exhausted. Would you like me to show you to your room?"

My room...for the night. It's just one night. Then, I'll find a way out of here. Ari and Drew will be fine. Alone time gave me an opportunity to plan my escape with Cyrus. He'd stayed away most of the day, but our bond told me he was close. I glanced around for Cyrus and saw him by the door. His face had an unreadable expression, and a pit formed in my stomach. "What about Cyrus? Where will he be?"

Laurel lifted a shoulder. "He's a unicorn. His laws are not ours. He can do as he wishes. As can you."

I doubted that. He had been generous and kind, but he hadn't let me out of his sight except to take care of personal needs. I hadn't seen unicorns though. The pit in my belly twisted. "Where are your unicorns in this kingdom?"

"My brother is one of the few who is linked with a unicorn. We can show Cyrus where she resides if that is comfortable for him."

Cyrus waited, giving me a soft smile.

I reached down the bond to him, savoring how the connection warmed. *You need to go be yourself. Tomorrow, we'll find a way to escape.*

You are right, Gemma, but I'm not leaving you here alone.

I don't trust Rainier, but I do trust Laurel. He could have done a million different things than he did today. I believe the goddesses and gods have a plan, and I'll be fine tonight. Maybe this will be the start of peace for our kingdoms.

He snorted. *Fine, but call for me if anything feels wrong. Anything.*

Cyrus exuded skepticism but also calm. Separation from him churned unease in my chest, but I couldn't pass up a chance to learn more about my mother...my history. *I promise.*

"I accept your offer to see the dwelling of the other unicorn on the premises," Cyrus said, giving Laurel a hard look.

"Very good. I'll have one of my men show you the way." He pulled out the little phone, a mobile phone he'd called it earlier, much smaller than the ones he showed me in various rooms, and tapped on the screen. He'd said those were called texts. "He'll meet us at the end of the hall. Shall we?"

Laurel held both hands out for me and helped me to my feet. The contact lit a fire under my skin. Then he directed us to the meeting spot. It was harder to say goodbye to Cyrus than I expected. It wasn't like this was a permanent parting, so why did it feel that way?

"I'll see you in the morning." I wrapped my arms around his neck and pulled him close. We didn't embrace often and less so the older I got. My body heated at the connection. *He's your bonded, Gemma. Stop it.*

He nuzzled against my neck. "Tomorrow."

Sparks tingled along my spine, and when we parted, I watched him until he disappeared around the corner. His steps grew quieter, and my heart sank.

"You promise nothing will happen to him, right?" I should have asked that before. He knew who I was so he knew my family had strong fae power. "Because if it does, I will rain down every bit of my magic on you personally before I tear your kingdom apart."

He took my hand in his and the fire sensation from earlier intensified. I tried to pull free, but his grip was strong. "I promise. I have no intention of hurting either of you. You are safe here. Both you and Cyrus."

Laurel's grip loosened on mine. I stopped fighting to free myself. His eyes softened as his gaze traveled down to our joined hands. He'd done nothing to threaten me or Cyrus, but he had insisted we stay. That one thing should be enough to make me run, but I didn't want to. Warmth spread between our hands in a way I'd never experienced. Maybe this was his magic. When he looked up again, I knew it wasn't. The same surprise was on his face as sparked inside me.

"Let me show you to your room." His voice was hoarse.

I worked on a swallow, and he watched my throat. "Yes, I'm ready for bed." *Goddesses and gods, why did I say that?* "I mean I'd like to rest."

My cheeks heated. My palm was damp, and I couldn't tell if it was my sweat or his or the heat between us causing it. I wanted to drag him to me and devour him, which seemed stupid considering the circumstances.

"I'll have your dinner brought to your room then, so you can rest." He traversed the maze of hallways with the memory of someone who had lived in the palace his whole life. He pointed to a door as we continued on the way. "This is my room.".

"Good to know." I smiled, committing it to memory but not venturing too close. He was a temptation I didn't need.

Laurel stopped at the next door. "And this is yours."

"So close to..." I let the words drift off. The distance seemed closer once I knew our rooms were next to each other in the hall.

"Only so I'm nearby if you need anything."

Oh, I needed something, but it wasn't separate rooms. It also wasn't something I should want from the enemy— no matter how nice he was.

"If it's okay with you, I'll come inside and show you

how a few things work—like the TV, phone, and water dispenser."

The way of living in the enemy empire was new to me and understanding it might help me figure a way out. "Yes, I'd like that."

He opened the door, and the lights came to life, illuminating the way.

"This works the TV." He held up a small rectangular box. "Press this button to turn it on and off."

The screen blinked on, and the sound was low like in the ones he'd shown me in the room with all the computers.

"To turn the sound up or down, you press this one, and push here to change the channel." He demonstrated both for me. "You have television in the bedroom, but don't stay up all night watching it. I want to show you something special in the morning, and we'll miss it if you sleep until noon."

Exhaustion seeped into every part of my body, but sleep in a foreign land where I was a prisoner seemed like a wistful thought. Laurel held out the remote, and our hands brushed as I took it from him. A shiver ran up my arm. *Space. I need space.* "I'm really tired, so I don't think that will be a problem."

"Right." He turned to the small kitchen area and retrieved a cup from the cabinet. "The water from the tap is fine to drink, but I recommend it from this filter." He slid the clear glass under a spout in a slim metal door. "It's much colder."

"Got it." I took the cup from him and took a sip. The chilled liquid cooled my heated insides. "It's good."

He smiled, opening the metal door. "There are some snacks like berries and cheese as well as juices if you want something else, but there will be a hot breakfast in the morning too."

I peered down to see my dress's crumpled fabric and dirty hem. Sweat beaded at the nape of my neck, and the scent of the forest clung to me. The modern surroundings of the palace awed me to the point that I hadn't realized I was a mess. "Where is the bathing chamber? I'd like to clean up."

"It's through there." He pointed into the room with the large bed. "The door on the left. The door next to the dresser is the closet. I had them bring in an assortment of clothes for you to choose from while we were touring the palace. I can send ladies to help you."

He seemed to think I'd be staying longer than one night, but I had a home to return to and siblings to hug.

"Thank you," I said, peeking into the bathroom. It was twice the size of the one in my kingdom, but the fixtures looked similar enough that I figured I could make do. "I can manage myself."

When I turned back to him, Laurel had reclined against the frame, holding out a piece of paper. "My phone number. You can just pick up any of the devices here and punch in the numbers in this order to reach me. You'll hear a ringing noise until I answer it." His gaze dipped to my mouth. "Or come to my door if you need anything."

It sounded simple enough. I reached for the slip of

paper. Our fingers brushed again, and an electric current sizzled through me. What was causing it?

"Walk me to the door?" He held his hand out for me.

I slipped mine in his and the warmth from earlier returned. This feeling was new and different and confusing.

He leaned forward—close enough to kiss me. The realization I wanted him to struck me deep in my core. I closed my eyes, anticipating his mouth on mine, but his lips brushed across my cheek instead and then against my ear. He whispered, "I'll see you in the morning."

My cheeks burned like the flames of a powerful fire wielder, knowing I'd misread his action, but also because I enjoyed the intimate touch as his lips met my skin.

"The morning, then," I whispered against his cheek.

CHAPTER 4

HER NAME
LAUREL

I let the steam fill the bathroom and imagined Gemma was doing the same thing. She was beautiful and smart, and I'd never felt so connected to a woman as I did her. Rain's duties prevented him from going on the mission this morning to check on the glamour General Daphina put in place for the prison. The scientists expected it to fail after her death like it had when she'd tried to leave initially, but it had stayed intact...only weakened with her passing ten years ago. When it started to gain strength, our experts suspected one of the daughters inherited her powers. Gemma's venture into the forest was fortunate. I'd never seen a woman more beautiful. As soon as I gazed into her eyes, I'd known who she was. She didn't seem to understand.

Then she'd played the piano with such passion, I was entranced. I'd fought back tears as her own ran down her cheeks. She was light in the darkness, and I desperately wanted to bask in her radiance.

Stepping into the shower, water flowed over me. I imagined what the blush on her cheeks would look like as I slipped my hands into her hair. She'd wanted me to kiss her at the door, and it took everything in me not to. I wouldn't have stopped at a kiss. She might have let me stay the night—maybe not, but she needed to know the truth first. The kingdom needed her here, and I wanted her by my side. Admitting that to myself made me falter. I gripped my cock and thought of how smooth her soft hand would be wrapped around it, stroking it up and down. I moved faster, chasing release of the desire pent-up in my balls.

With her name on my lips, my orgasm came hard and fast. I watched while my cock throbbed as it spurted fluid on the wall and wished it had been all over her perfect tits. Goddesses and gods, I'd been so hard for her just from a few touches. What would it be like to fuck her? She was going to ruin me, and I wanted her to. I prayed it would happen soon.

I pulled the showerhead loose and pointed it toward the dark chevron tile, washing my seed down the drain. The staff didn't need to find that on the wall tomorrow. Gemma's long auburn hair flashed through my mind—the way it flew over her shoulders when she turned her head. Her beauty shimmered with light beyond this realm, but it was her fearless nature and inquisitive mind that intrigued me. Something deep inside me needed to delve deeper to understand her, even beyond my empath abilities. I finished my shower, toweled off, and slid on some loose clothes.

A knock at the door had me rolling my eyes. I knew who it was before I even got there.

I opened the door, but not too wide. "Hello, Brother."

"She's in her room?" He peered around me into my suite.

"Most people greet the person in return." I crossed my arms, annoyed by his insinuation that I'd bed Gemma without giving her time to adjust or showing her the true history of the war.

Rain stared at me blinking. He wore his training leathers, but he was sweating, so he hadn't been sparring. Given the hour, that meant he must have been interrupted on his way.

I pushed the door open farther for him to enter. "Yes, she's in her room. Did you expect me to be a bastard the first night?"

"Like me, you mean," he said, dropping onto the couch. Guilt gouged between my shoulder blades. He'd taken plenty of hits over his reputation with the social sites—some deserved, but most weren't.

"That's not what I meant." I sat on the other end. "What's this visit about?"

"The vampires are pushing the border again, so I'm leaving the day after tomorrow to join the troops there."

My chest twisted like it did every time he went to the front. It had nothing to do with him being the ruler and everything to do with being my brother. He didn't look worried, but the attacks on our borders were becoming a regular thing. The vampires tested us for weaknesses to get to their false king. Our line held. The frequency of the

CROWN OF BROKEN PROMISES   33

skirmishes was a concern. "And you're sure it's necessary?"

"They need my leadership and my particular skills."

I nodded. His power was particularly useful against vampires, especially when there were a lot of them. My skills were less useful for fighting the enemy but more so for the injured and gauging the mood. "I can be ready to go by then. I'll need to rearrange plans for Gemma."

"No, you stay here. That task is as important as holding that border."

"She's not a task." I growled out the words. Gemma was a member of our people and far more than a chore. "She's fae."

He held his hands up. "Of course. I didn't mean it as an insult."

I relaxed against the couch, sinking into the cushions. Gemma made me want to defend her, but I had a feeling she didn't need my protection. She might even be pissed if I tried to. "Sorry. I'm—"

"Frustrated?"

My cheeks heated. Despite having jerked off in the shower, I was, in fact, filled with need for her.

"I think you have a little competition with her bonded judging by the way he was so possessive earlier."

"You noticed that too, huh?" I liked how protective he was of her. Gemma felt safe with him, and she needed the security, especially with what I had to eventually tell her.

"I did. I didn't think that was allowed in their kingdom."

"Same." Cyrus was incredibly striking in his human

form. I couldn't blame Gemma if she was fucking him. Hell, if I weren't so consumed by her, I might pursue Cyrus. The way my body heated around her, and even more so when she threatened to use her magic on me and tear down this kingdom if I harmed her bonded, was unusual. There was something different about what was going on between us. Even if I didn't know exactly what it was, I was sure she was attracted to me too. I shook my head. A hard-on wasn't what I needed at the moment, and it would be fuel for my brother to tease me with. "Are you sure you don't want me to go with you to the front? These pushes are becoming more frequent from the vampires."

Rain picked at the fabric on the arm of the couch. He was more concerned than he was saying. "They are after something. We don't know what yet, so we must hold them at bay."

"You know what it is, Rain. We both do. The elders do. Anyone alive from that time knows." He wasn't fooling me, and I wasn't sure why he didn't say it out loud. It was just us in my room, but it was like he was just as afraid as the others to utter the false king's name—as if speaking it would break the spell and allow him to vanyshen in front of us.

"The magic didn't die with Daphina, so there has to be another aspect we are missing."

I sighed. The power would fail eventually, and the entire realm would be in danger. "We need to be prepared for when it does fail."

"That's why you must stay and persuade Gemma to remain here and help. It was luck that brought you to her, but the rest is up to you now. She clearly didn't care for me."

I laughed. Luck seemed to have nothing to do with it. I'd call it more fate, but I wasn't ready to admit that to anyone. "Can you blame her? Not many people like you."

He smirked. "Perks of the job." My brother studied me for a long moment, and I saw the fear he kept hidden from everyone else. "You really like her. A lot."

"That's a bit of a stretch. I literally met her today," I said. She'd expected me to kiss her, but her relationship with her bonded seemed like more. I wouldn't step between them if that was true. "And if the unicorn is who she seeks instead, I will respect that."

"Maybe she wants you to fight for her." Rain returned to picking at the fabric.

"Hmm... I didn't take you for a romantic, Brother." I contemplated that, but Gemma didn't seem like that type of woman. "Maybe she doesn't know what she wants."

"Yet," Rain said. "You need to show her."

I stared up at the ceiling. What I had planned for tomorrow could, likely would, be emotional. Contrition climbed up my back and wrapped around my throat. "I'm taking her to the statue tomorrow."

He looked skeptical. "That's pretty quick. Are you sure she's ready? To venture out into the city?"

I thought about how well Gemma had accepted all the things I'd shown her today. Her ability to acclimate so quickly to new things was impressive. "She's picked up on all the tech here like it's second nature. My gut says she'll be just fine."

"A natural."

"She's intelligent and strong and..."

"Fuckable?"

My brother saying it soured my stomach. Yes, Gemma was as fuckable as women came, but she was more than that. Maybe not more for me. The way our family treated the people they cared about was by poisoning them for the good of the kingdom or even by execution at times. It wasn't a place for someone like Gemma. Rain and I survived because we came back from the war and many of our family didn't. When the King's cousin, Laveena, murdered him our aunt, Queen Edwina, abdicated the throne with no surviving children, she passed it on to our father. He'd been weary after my mother's death on the battlefield that was now a forest of trapped souls, but when he'd heard Rain had been gravely injured in an offensive to push the vampires back, Father had gone across the Vampire Kingdom border with no guards. Father never became king as a fae prince cannot claim the throne unmarried. I shook my head to cast away the memory. If I'd been there instead of performing funeral rituals on the battlefield between the prison kingdom and ours... Rain and I had lost almost our entire family, but our bond as brothers was forged on the battlefield and not in the blood we shared.

That didn't mean I'd let him talk about Gemma as 'fuckable' though. "Maybe we shouldn't speak of her like that out of respect for her and Daphina."

He smirked at me. "How do you think she would react to know that her mother held the late king's favor?"

The love letters King Veran had written to General Daphina were archived at a museum under the care of a historian and friend of Daphina. Gemma acclimated with ease to everything I introduced her to today, but no one deserved to be blindsided by their family history. If she agreed to stay, I'd help guide her through the details and at a pace she dictated. "That conversation is a long way off. We have a lot of milestones to clear before she'll be ready to hear that kind of history."

"She's made you different in one day. I wonder how soft you'll be when I return." He slapped my arm.

I'd had my fill of his retorts. "Get out of my room, Rain." I stood and walked toward the door. "Now."

My brother laughed all the way to the doorway and stopped. "Does Merrick know?"

I cringed at my ex-lover's name. Merrick had been so jealous when I brought a woman to bed with us. Our entire relationship was supposed to be a no-strings thing, but then Merrick caught feelings. Feelings I didn't share. "Know what?"

"That you love her."

I shoved my brother into the hall. "Fuck off, Rain."

He was laughing harder, slapping his leg.

I chuckled. "You're an asshole." Movement next to us caught my eye. Gemma stood in a flimsy nightgown barely covered by a matching robe. *Goddesses and gods, strike me down dead now.*

She glanced between us like we were monsters. Rain, for his part, recovered quicker. He inclined his head toward her and walked away, leaving us alone. She looked more beautiful than when I saw her in the woods.

"I'm sorry if we disturbed you. Did you need something?" I tried to keep my voice calm and hoped she didn't hear the waver in it. "I arranged for you to have help in the morning to dress. I forgot to tell you earlier."

"No." She shook her head. "No. No. I'm good." She spun on her heels and marched toward her door.

"I'll let them know they won't be needed."

Fucking hell. I knew damn well it wasn't because of the ladies to dress her. She probably thought we were two stupid fae joking about her future. Everything in me said to chase after her, but I forced myself back into my room. She needed to know her space was hers, and I wouldn't invade it without her permission.

CHAPTER 5
CHOCOLATE & DEALS
GEMMA

I leaned against the back of my door, letting the coolness soothe my embarrassment. Goddesses and gods, how had I been so stupid? I put on this stupid nightgown to go scratch the itch he'd burned under my skin. He was in love with someone named Merrick. I smacked my forehead as if that would remove this nightmare from my memories. *Fuck.*

"Urggh." I was such an idiot for thinking he wanted me. He probably acted like that with every fucking woman. "I'm leaving tomorrow. I'll tell Cyrus first thing."

Shaking my head for talking to myself, I opened the cold box to look for a snack. On the colder side was a container of ice cream. We'd had it for special occasions growing up, but never from a container. There was one marked vanilla and one chocolate.

Definitely the chocolate. If ever there was a night for it...

I rummaged through the drawers until I found a spoon and headed to the couch with the carton. The lid came off easily and the chocolate scent floated up as I inhaled. I dug the spoon in and took a big bite.

Sitting on the blue sofa, I turned on the TV with the little box and flipped through the channels like Laurel had shown me. I scooped out another spoonful of the ice cream, but it was too big. A cold headache spread to my temples. I grabbed my head and held a breath of hot air in my mouth. The pain subsided.

The show I'd been watching on unicorns ended. I'd only seen a few minutes of the program, but apparently, a few unicorns remained near the kingdom's cities. Most of their kind on this side of the forest had relocated to the far side of the lands. The voice talking over the videos gave no reason. I picked up the remote and paused. The people on TV talked about Laurel and how he taught healing skills to the school students. An image of him crouched down with a child, both smiling, flashed on the screen. It was endearing to see him interact with the people so easily. His kingdom loved him by all accounts. Some women were acting like he was a newborn baby unicorn deserving of all this attention, not that one of those had been born recently. I assumed the same was true in Laurel's kingdom as mine.

Not wanting to look at his face anymore, I hit the button to change the channel. I sighed. Staring back at me were Laurel and Rainier. Each of the men shook hands and chatted with their people. The clear difference came in the response the citizens had to them. Although the crowd maintained respect, they were more formal and maybe a bit fearful of Rainier. With Laurel, faces lit up with genuine smiles, and his in return. As they made their way into a large building, finely clothed people greeted them. Laurel kissed the cheek of a beautiful woman with long, wavy, brown hair. Her high cheekbones brightened with a pink tinge on her pale skin. I clicked the power button, and the screen went dark as he entered the building with her on his arm.

I tossed the remote across the couch and left it there. *Is that the woman he loves?* She was striking, and they looked good together. That had to be Merrick. I wanted to use my wind magic to propel myself home through the forest. I wasn't staying, so why did it bother me? I couldn't have him either way. The enemy prince belonged to another in his kingdom, which was as it should be. The problem was that I liked him. I crooked my finger to close the bedroom door with wind magic, and it slammed harder than I meant it to. The reverberation vibrated the walls. Everyone on the floor probably heard the noise. *Fucking goddesses and gods.* My stupidity mounted with each second I spent here.

I stood at the window and stared out at the darkened city lit by the moonlight and the lights powered by electricity. It was quieter now than when Laurel showed me the view from the other side of the palace and explained cars to me. I wanted to drive a car, but that wouldn't happen since I wasn't staying. This wasn't the first time I liked a guy who liked someone else, but it was the first time I suspected it was serious. It had to be. Rainier had asked Laurel if Merrick knew he was in love with her. He wouldn't have said that if it wasn't more than a fling.

Goddesses and gods, Gemma. You've known this man for less than a day. He's in love with someone else. Walk the fuck away. This will only end up in getting your feelings hurt. You aren't staying.

A couple strolled hand-in-hand along the path below, and I imagined them as me and Laurel, remembering the warmth between our hands when we touched. I let out a long breath. *No. Erase that little dream right now.*

I walked into the bathing chamber and splashed cold water on my face. After patting it dry, I pulled the plush covers back on the bed and punched one of the thick pillows. The contact reminded me of training and gave me some relief. I punched it again and a few more times and imagined it was the manifestation of the foolish schoolgirl crush I had on my captor.

My need to pummel my feelings satisfied, I tossed the throw pillows across the room and climbed into bed with a smile on my face.

Sun drifted in through the windows. It was the early morning light that bathed everything in oranges that turned pink. I'd been dreaming of Laurel. It was bad enough to have to face him today after showing up in that nightgown, but even worse, he had been in my dreams doing exactly what I wanted him to do.

I regretted not accepting Laurel's offer to send ladies to help me dress. The clothes were different, and I thought about what I'd seen the citizens wearing on the TV last night. Choosing some pants that had a little hook-and-bar closure at the waist and a zipper, I paired them with a purple blouse and black trousers similar to what the host of the show last night wore. I bathed and dressed quickly, staring at myself in the mirror. "You are a strong and smart woman, and you don't need him or any other man."

A knock rapped at the door, and I jumped. The place had my nerves on edge. It made me jumpy because, at home, there was very little I was frightened by.

I flung the door open, and Laurel smiled in the same way I'd seen him do on the TV last night. He seemed like such a contradiction, and I didn't know which part was real.

"Are you ready for breakfast?" he asked while gesturing to the woman with the cart behind him.

I opened the door wider and forced myself to smile. "Where's Cyrus?"

My bonded hadn't invaded my thoughts, but I hadn't tried him either. The quiet in my mind was a nice change given what was going through it last night.

A bit of disappointment flashed across his face. "He should be here anytime."

The lady with him rolled the cart into the living room. Her mouth gaped open. I followed her gaze to the sticky goop on the counter.

"Oh, the ice cream. I forgot about it."

"It's no problem," the woman responded with a smile.

"It is," I said, embarrassed to make an untidy impression. "I'm not usually so messy. I can clean it up...once I figure out where the supplies are."

"No, I've got it. I'll set your breakfast up on the table instead." She went to work quickly, putting plates and bowls out. Help had been available at my every whim in my kingdom, so I should be used to the response, but it bothered me that she felt obligated to do so.

Curiosity danced through Laurel's eyes as he studied me. "Did you watch TV last night?"

"Some," I said, recalling the images of him and the magnificent Merrick. "But it got obnoxious."

"I don't watch it much." He dropped into a seat at the table. "But there are sporting events and a couple of shows I try to catch."

"Sporting events? What do they consist of?" I sat in one of the chairs across from him. The light glinted off his eyes, and they transitioned from a warm honey color to a coppery hue. The way they shifted was like a forgotten enchantment danced.

"Some allow for magic, and some don't. It's the latter I prefer. We play a game called Moirai, after the Fates. No magic can be used."

"Interesting." Not many in my kingdom would participate in an event where they couldn't use their powers. "Why do you prefer those?"

"It puts everyone on an even playing field. A win is well earned." He smiled, and it was warm like the sun breaking through the curtains.

His genuineness made me like him despite the fact he was in love with this Merrick person, and I couldn't afford that. Maybe if he wasn't with her...it didn't matter because he was. Liking Laurel would lead down a road of heartbreak. I needed to get back to my kingdom and my family. "I'd like to leave today. Preferably as soon as Cyrus is here. I'm sure my siblings and Father are missing me, and I am most certainly missing them."

Laurel's face dropped in disappointment. "As I mentioned yesterday, there is something I'd like to show you. I'll not force you to stay, but I'll escort you home myself if you'll indulge me on this outing."

I needed distance from him because I wanted to say yes to everything that came out of his mouth. That wasn't me. Getting home to my sister and brother had to be the priority. Staying would cross a line, and I pushed away from the table determined to not fall for his kindness. "I'd prefer to go now. When will Cyrus be here?"

"He should be here anytime now." Laurel wrapped his hand around mine.

The touch was magnetic. It was like I couldn't let go... not that I wanted to. The connection melted in like it seeped through the skin-to-skin contact. *He's in love with someone else, Gemma.* Still, I couldn't let go.

Cyrus? Where are you?

They're leading me down a hallway where your room is supposed to be. You do know this is the royal wing?

I figured that Laurel's room was next door.

Did he...touch you?

He was touching me right now, but it seemed too intimate to share that with Cyrus. I opted for the piece of the truth I could share. *He's been a complete gentleman.*

Good. I'd hate to have to spear him with my horn and start another war.

I bit down on my lip to keep from laughing out loud. *Maybe we just focus on getting home and not starting wars.*

Deal.

I pulled my hand free of Laurel, and he studied me.

He looked like he was choosing his words carefully. "What can I say for you to agree to take the walk with me this morning?"

There was one thing I very much wanted to do that I couldn't do back home. "If you let me drive one of the car things, I'll go see whatever it is you want to show me."

"Deal." The irony that he responded with the same thing Cyrus had said about war would have been comical if I hadn't just agreed to spend more time with a prince of the enemy kingdom.

CHAPTER 6

MOTHER

GEMMA

The light had shifted to the midmorning sun as we stepped onto the sidewalk beyond the palace. Cyrus was on one side of me and Laurel on the other. They crowded in on me, but I couldn't walk faster since I didn't know where we were going.

Thank you for not fighting me on this.

If he's taking you where I suspect, I support this excursion.

I hoped it was to drive a car, but no one knew that. *Any hints?*

No, if I'm right, you need the full impact of it. His amicable demeanor surprised me. I expected him to suggest we use this time to escape.

Laurel had refused to give me hints too. It was like the two of them actually got along...at least on one topic.

I narrowed my gaze at Cyrus. *You are my bonded. Why are you helping the prince of our enemy kingdom?*

I'm your bonded, and I will die for you if it means you live. I'm also a unicorn, and we don't answer to fae.

Though I wasn't bound by the oath Cyrus was, I'd give my life for him too. That didn't change the fact that he'd used the response he gave when he didn't want to answer. *That's a bit of a horseshit-nothing response.*

We...Unicorns know things because our lines are not divided by the boundary of a kingdom.

So, you knew how this kingdom had thrived since the war. The advancements of the enemy kingdom exceeded ours in ways I couldn't have imagined. Why had our historians told us the enemy was nearly wiped from the realm when they were flourishing?

Yes, not all, but I did. I haven't been here since before you were born. It has changed much since that time.

And where we are headed?

Was constructed at the end of the war. Unicorn and fae built it together. It's very...special.

Seriously? The frustration built in me, and I wanted to show him I remembered all of our sparring matches.

Completely.

I'm kicking your ass later.

A rough laugh came down our bond. He was amused, but there was something else in the rasp of it that made my cheeks burn. Something I'd wanted to explore but I knew was forbidden, so I jammed the thought to the back of my mind. Thankfully, the sun shining on us was an excellent excuse for flushed cheeks.

Remember your training as we head into the space.

Why—

"It's just around the corner," Laurel said, cutting off my thoughts. A sweet smile spread over his face like that of a kid with an excellent secret. "There will be a number of people there given the time of year, but they likely will not see the resemblance after the decades that have passed."

"What do you mean?" *Did he mean they won't recognize him?* That seemed unlikely they wouldn't given how I'd seen the people react on the TV and the number of guards with us.

I set my shield up in anticipation of the large number of people. We rounded the corner into a bustling intersection with multiple streets, a dozen if my count was right, ending in a circle around a statue. The figure appeared female from this angle, but I couldn't make out the features. Confused by what he deemed so important he'd brought me to this crowded street to show me a statue, I almost tripped over a bouquet. I peered around the scene. So many flowers and wreaths and people on their knees praying lined the way. Laurel guided us around the statue toward the front. People elbowed each other and moved out of the way, but they didn't try to approach. They gave him the space our entire party needed to navigate.

"Why are there so many here today? Is this normal?"

"There were more yesterday, and many make the pilgrimage this week."

I didn't remember any celebrations on this day or this week in my kingdom, and since Mother died, it had been a time of mourning. *What are they observing?*

"Look up," he whispered in my ear when we made it to the front.

My gaze traveled up the statue of a woman until I

landed on a face I knew in my heart and my memories. I mashed my lips together to hold back a sob. My eyes burned with tears. "That's my mother."

"It is," Laurel confirmed.

Cyrus, in his human form, placed a steadying hand on my lower back.

Mother...without a doubt, it was her likeness. Disbelief fought the truth my eyes beheld. My chest hollowed and filled at the same time. I pressed a hand over my heart to remind myself to breathe. The woman who raised me, who taught me to play the piano, who taught me to be fierce and kind, stood in a place of reverence among a people I'd been raised to hate.

"How? Why?" I found a plaque, and through my blurred vision, I read *General Daphina—Chosen by Nyx*.

Mother's destiny was memorialized here, and I didn't know anything about her history. *General...and Nyx's chosen?* Her magic...I'd known she'd been powerful, but not gifted by the Goddess herself. *What else did I not know about those I love? The war?*

As people parted, more plaques lined the base and the ground as etched testimonies. Flowers upon flowers covered more. Those blessed moonflowers Mother taught Ari to grow in their special garden grew here...were in so many of the bouquets. The white flowers Ari had cultivated. That would be maddening to my sister. A smile curled my lips as I knelt at the statue. Tears streamed down as I laid my hand on the plaque with Mother's name and gazed up at the massive stone likeness.

Mother hadn't just lived here. It had been her home before the war and what she meant when she told me to look for her in the woods. She meant her people. Our people. The stories she'd shared with me so many times were true, and I reached for those memories in desperation for the knowledge. This place with so many fae was meant to be our home. My siblings and I, raised to hate the kingdom on the other side of the forest, were taught falsehoods instead of the truth. But Father...he must have known. Why hadn't he brought us here? If for no other reason, he should have allowed Ari and I to mourn our mother here with her people. A sob tore through me. Was I actually the enemy of my kingdom embedded like a tick? Warmth flanked both my sides—Cyrus on one and Laurel on the other. They knelt with me. We stayed in that position for so long that I lost track of time. The cobblestones below dug into my skin through the pants.

I swallowed against the knot and cleared my throat, focusing on the question I wondered at our arrival. "They come on this week and yesterday because they know my mother is gone?"

"Many have come since the statue was built, but this week is a week of remembrance in her honor and has been for the last decade," he said, his tone quiet.

My chest twisted in waves of grief mixed with gratitude. As I'd placed flowers at the edge of the forest each anniversary of her death, Mother's people had come here to honor her. She was not forgotten like the horrible forest.

"Gemma," Cyrus said, his voice soft like a breeze and close to my ear. "I'm not trying to rush you, but I don't think they will stand until you do."

I glanced over my shoulder to see fae on their right knees with their right arms over their chests—hands resting against the left shoulder. Heads bowed. They gave my mother reverence, not a bow we observed in my kingdom, but it clearly was one in this place. Mother had been loved here...was still loved here. I choked back another sob and worked a swallow to loosen the knot in my throat. My composure in check to the poise we were raised to carry, I stood.

Heads of fae I didn't know met my gaze. Their act of veneration temporarily robbed me of speech, so I reached for their hands instead. I took as many as I could, alternating sides. Laurel stood close to me, and Cyrus placed a hand low on my back as we made our way through the crowd. Laurel waved the guards off to give room for people to share the moment. So many had tears in their eyes. Thanks were muttered to me, and I didn't know what for. I'd done nothing in the war. I hadn't even been born until long after the Great War ended. Then, it occurred to me they were thanking me for my mother's sacrifice, and my tears mixed with theirs. They had lost her even before I had...probably lost family of their own.

Laurel had his phone out, and I saw him punch some letters in before putting it back in his pocket. The guards flanked us as we crossed the street and sound returned around me. I hadn't even realized how quiet it had gotten.

Shouts came from behind us. A woman stood ahead,

tears in her eyes, and pressed her hand over her heart. Her lip trembled. "Daughter of Daphina, you are our daughter. A daughter of this land." The woman's voice wavered. "Her magic and sacrifice live on in you."

"So much for not being recognized," I muttered and poked Laurel in the ribs with my elbow.

He winced, but his lips ghosted up in a smile. "I didn't know you were going to make a spectacle of yourself like that."

The crowd moved in our direction. "Maybe if someone had warned me I was going to see a statue of my dead mother, I might have been more prepared."

"Noted. I'll take the blame."

"Since you kidnapped me— "

"I did not. I strongly suggested, but you have been free to do as you please."

I rolled my eyes. "Semantics, Laurel." I looked over my shoulder to see the crowd following us. "This is getting a little overwhelming."

"We have a ride ahead that will take us back to the palace."

I blew out a breath. "Good. Because I have questions for you." I glanced at Cyrus. "Both of you."

It hurt to know that Mother had an entire life before our kingdom. I knew very little, if anything, about that life, but it was freeing to know she hadn't been losing her mind when she told me stories of this city. Here she'd been more than a queen of a fae kingdom. She'd made a differ-ence. I looked back, taking the statue in one more time, and slipped into the car. Cyrus slid in next to me, and

Laurel sunk into the seat on my other side, so I was sand-wiched in between them. Having them on either side comforted me. I looked out the window at the people gathered there. My mother's people. My people. A people who bowed in respect for my mother's sacrifice and not as if I was the enemy princess.

CHAPTER 7

THE MUSEUM
LAUREL

The car lurched to a start, and I let out a breath. Rain and I were used to those kinds of crowds, but Gemma hadn't been in that kind of position in Albert's prison. Casimir limited the information she obtained, but our volunteers hadn't. I wanted to kick myself for not anticipating the crowd's reaction, but I'd felt the emotion pouring out of them when they recognized her. Gemma couldn't even speak. It must have been overwhelming. *Goddesses and gods, did I fuck up not telling her we were going to her mother's statue?* I wanted to kiss every tear she shed away, but a sign of affection like that would have made every news station in the kingdom. Gemma didn't need to be a target for Merrick and her bullshit either, and that was a sure way Merrick would invite herself for a visit to the palace. Her father had introduced us in hopes we would marry, but not too long after I slept with her, the darker side of her came out. She was powerful and ruthless, and I didn't want her anywhere near Gemma.

I placed my hand on Gemma's knee and squeezed. She looked at me with red-rimmed eyes. "Thank you for today. It was hard. A part of me feels broken, like my mother must have felt living in our kingdom, but I feel free of a lie I didn't know my life was built on."

Reassurance was what she needed from me, and I'd give her every bit of it I could. "This is your kingdom. It always has been. You just didn't know."

"I have so many questions. Are there historical accounts of my mother I can read?"

I nodded. The historians had retained records meticulously to preserve the sacrifice her mother made. "There are, and there are some first-hand stories I can arrange for you to hear as well."

She let go of a massive breath. "I want all of it. Every bit of information there is about her. She'd told me stories when she got sick, and I thought it was the illness stealing her reality. She'd chosen me to tell those stories to because she couldn't tell anyone else. If others can help confirm those, I'd welcome a visit with them."

Gemma agreed to stay to learn more, so the trip to the statue paid off. I wondered at what cost. Not all of our history painted the picture of epic heroism like General Daphina.

"Your mother was more than a general to the people here," Cyrus said. "The unicorn considered her a friend, and that is not a term our kind uses lightly."

What Cyrus shared was true. Daphina was a loss to all,

but to none more than the king. That news might come as a shock to her to know King Veran cared for her mother as the general did him. His first wife had died in childbirth along with their unborn child. No one knew where either were buried. In his grief, he'd had their interment shrouded with secrecy. Some say his descent into madness began then, but those of us close to the palace knew it was when he'd been forced to let Daphina go and choose another, my aunt. When Daphina rose to prominence at university, she gained his attention both for her beauty and her mind. No one would ever reach his heart again. "Both fae and unicorn knew the loss of General Daphina. She's not just a hero of the war but *the* hero of the war."

Gemma

EACH NEW PIECE of information was like a punch to the gut, knocking the wind out of me. So many questions swirled in my mind, and I wanted answers to them all. "But how? What did she do, and why did she and Father choose to live basically in exile across the border? Why did they not visit here?"

"That's a long story, and perhaps better told where I can show you some of the historical records." His gaze shifted to the driver. "Armstrong, take us to the War Museum."

The man met Laurel's gaze in the little mirror and

nodded. He turned down a street in a different direction, and I stared out the window. The buildings separated by green spaces flew by in a blur. Cars were exhilarating. Laurel had promised that if I stayed for his excursion, and I'm grateful I did, I could learn how to steer a car.

"I want to drive."

Cyrus tensed beside me.

Laurel gave me an easy smile. "Let's try that in a smaller vehicle first. They are easier to maneuver than a big one like this."

It made sense. When we learned to ride, we started on ponies before horses. "Fine, but it has to be today." Because I was leaving afterward. I'd give myself this one experience to take home as a memory.

"If you are still up for it after the museum, I'll let you drive one of my cars."

"I'll agree to that," I said, excited for new adventures. I realized I wasn't afraid. My grief, my grief still on my palate, made it difficult to delight fully in the new experiences. But with Laurel the exhilaration magnified and pulled me in so deep I thought I might drown in it. "How far is the museum?"

"Not far. Maybe five or ten minutes depending on traffic."

The area we were in was busier than some of the other streets. I left my shield in place, so auras didn't bombard me.

"I don't think this is a good idea," Cyrus said. The concern rolled down our bond. "Gemma only learned of her mother's role today. She was safeguarded from the secrets of the war by Daphina's choice."

He wanted to keep me safe, but I wasn't the teenager from before he'd bonded me. The world was much bigger, and I didn't want to live in fear of it. "I'm done being protected, Cyrus. I want to know the truth, and if those answers are at this museum, then that is where I'm going."

Laurel cleared his throat in what suspiciously sounded like him covering a laugh. I buried my elbow in his ribs.

"Oof," he said. "Not necessary."

"Gemma, you do not know what you are going to find."

"But you do." I pointed an accusing finger at him. "And so do you." I turned my finger on Laurel. "Do you understand what it's like for everyone around you to know more about your family than you do?"

Both of them went silent.

"At least Laurel is offering the means for me to learn where I come from. What have you done, Cyrus? Except go along with the lies?" His betrayal stung more than it should. The attraction I'd kept hidden made it worse. Unicorns didn't answer to fae as he liked to remind me. *Fucking unicorns.*

His voice thundered into my head. *It's not like that, Gemma, and you should know that. There is more to it. First and foremost, I protect you—physically, mentally, and in any other way required.*

I refused to reply through our bond. "If you don't want to be part of this, then you can get out of the car now."

"Maybe we stop the car first if he wants to get out." Laurel leaned around me.

I narrowed my gaze at him. "Do you want another elbow?"

"No, ma'am." He held a hand up and sank into the seat.

The car hit a bump, jostling me around. I scrambled to grab something, my hand landed on Laurel's thigh. *Way too close to his...* I jerked my hand back to my lap and swallowed hard.

"Back to you." I looked at Cyrus. "Are you staying, or do you want out?"

He didn't cower. A unicorn wouldn't. "I'm staying, of course. I wouldn't leave you, Gemma."

My heart thrummed at the declaration, but I wouldn't back down either. "Then not another word or even a suggestion of keeping any more secrets from me. Are we clear?"

"I will not keep any fae secrets from you," he said.

"Good enough." Unicorns didn't answer to us, so it truly was the best he could do. His concession to give me that promise was something unicorns did with friends, and that meant a lot to me...but I was still agitated with him.

CHAPTER 8

THE CURATOR
LAUREL

The car came to a stop in front of the museum, and Cyrus's warning made me second-guess my decision. Not going in would shield Gemma from the pain, but she deserved to know the truth. If it were me, I'd want to know, and my gut told me Gemma would too.

I held my hand out to help her from the car. She looked at my open palm and up to my eyes. Her gaze burned into me. My dick jerked as if she'd seen right to it. She liked me whether she wanted to admit it or not, and I liked her. That might all change after the museum. Seeing your mother as a hero was one thing. Seeing the devastation of the war was another. Seeing the evidence of a father's betrayal was life-changing.

Her hand slid into mine, and I relished the instant heat of our connection. Cyrus made a noise like a growl. I didn't know unicorns could make a sound like that. I glanced and him and smiled. He was in his human form, and his face was bright red. I stopped short of chuckling, not wanting to be on the receiving end of another fierce elbow from Gemma.

Armstrong held open the door to the most modern-looking building in the kingdom. It reminded me of some of the buildings in the human realm. I'd often question why the angular design had been chosen, but the copper with its natural patina from the years since construction consumed less energy. The two-story windows in the front filled the lobby with natural light and harvested it, so that the building functioned without dependency on magic or alternate energy.

Whit, the exhibit manager, hurried toward us. Several hundred years my senior, I'd known the tall fae my entire life, and he'd had gray hair all that time. He bowed at the waist. "Your Highness, I wasn't expecting you today."

"Whit, we are friends. You do not need to bow or be formal in front of my friends."

Whit's gaze traveled over my companions and back to me. A hint of confusion flashed in his eyes, but he smiled warmly. "Yes, Laurel. It's always good to see you. What brings you to the museum today?"

I debated on how to introduce Gemma, but the news of who she was would be on the social gossip sites by now and the local stations later. "This is Gemma, daughter of General Daphina. She is accompanied by her bonded unicorn, Cyrus."

Whit's eyebrows rose halfway to his receding hairline. He was one of our oldest citizens and a treasured historian, but in all his centuries of living, he had never learned to cover his emotions. He took Gemma's hand in his and patted it. "You are the very image of her. I didn't realize you'd joined us, or I would have come to you. You must have many questions."

Gemma, for her part, gave him a warm, easy smile as if she'd run into a family friend. "I do. I'm hoping Laurel brought me to you for those answers. Did you know my mother?"

"Yes, indeed. Your mother and I were great friends before the war, and I knew your father as well."

Gemma's father was the subject I was most concerned with her hearing. No matter what we showed her, she knew a different man than we were about to reveal. Initially, I worried she wouldn't believe the truth, but my concern shifted to her being devastated by how truly evil the man she'd grown up with was. "Gemma has only heard a tiny bit of her mother's history and none of her father's. Maybe we can ease into the latter topic and focus on her mother first."

Whit nodded. "Of course. Let me ask one of the attendants to cover the front and hold any visitors, and we can start with a private tour."

A young fae who looked familiar, but I was certain I hadn't seen before, showed up to the front counter. He studied us, and the sternness of his stare made me curious about him. His stare lingered on Gemma, and I angled my body between them. He shifted his focus to the computer like it was more interesting. His features reminded me of someone, but I couldn't figure out who. Could he be the son of a noble I hadn't seen in years? That had to be the answer.

"Ready?" Whit asked.

"Yes," Gemma answered and linked her arm through his.

Whit smiled at her and patted her arm the same way he had her hand. He had that effect on people, and the connection was more than his empathic abilities. Although Whit's empath skills were greater than mine, he'd taught me how to expand them. I'd leaned toward the physical healing magic whereas he was more focused on emotions.

Cyrus must not have been threatened by Whit the way he was me because he didn't make any attempts to intervene. They both fought in the war, so maybe their paths had crossed. Whit was well-liked among the unicorns as the war ended, perhaps before then too. Maybe Cyrus knew of the stories or maybe he saw what I did in Whit. He was a genuinely good person.

When we were out of earshot of the young man at the desk, I moved closer to Whit. "Who is the kid working for you? I haven't seen him before."

"Apologies. I assumed you knew," he said, his eyes widening slightly. "He's a cousin of Lady Merrick's."

Fuck. Of course. I should have figured that out. I met him when he was like five.

Gemma stiffened, and I wasn't sure what had her reacting like that. With Cyrus on one side and Whit on the other, I couldn't comfort her. I held in the groan forming in my chest. The young man would surely report back to

Merrick, and she would petition a visit with some fabri-
cated request as a guise to inflict cruelty. That couldn't
happen, but I'd worry about stopping her in a way that
wouldn't piss her father off later. My focus needed to be
on Gemma while we were in the exhibit.

CHAPTER 9

THE PAINTING

W hit's kind gaze landed on me, and he launched into an unpracticed spiel. I appreciated he didn't give me the generic version for the masses. According to the counter we passed, over a million people had entered the museum, and I wasn't sure if that was a million this month, year, or what time period. The figure was incomprehensible. My entire kingdom probably had a tenth of that number.

"Your mother and I knew each other for a long time. We both served in King Veran's court after college—higher education studies. From a young age, she displayed a brilliant strategic mind that only improved in college. Your father stood out in strategy as well, and that's how they became friends."

Confused by his account, I reached out to stop him. "They met in this secondary school? They had told us they knew each other as kids."

"We'll get to how that story came about." Whit

gestured toward a wall of the exhibit. "Your mother won many battles in the war, and the king chose to honor her by promoting her to general."

My heart tightened with the freshness of the reverence I observed at Mother's statue. Cyrus and Laurel stood behind us like sentries, and as I reached down the bond with Cyrus, I met resistance.

Patience. Whit will tell your family history better than I can.

Whit cleared his throat. "The battles she won held the vampires at the border and kept them from invading our lands until they garnered inside help."

Shock waved over me like a blot of magic. "Inside help? You mean from fae?"

"You don't seem shocked by vampires," Whit said, cocking an eyebrow.

While the stories I'd been told referred to them primarily as the nosferatu, I knew of the vampires' existence, but I'd been told they had no way to enter our lands. "No, some of the stories Mother told me were about them, but she never said there was help from fae for them to gain access to our empire."

Laurel moved closer, followed by Cyrus. The protectiveness smothered me, but I was thankful to have them both nearby.

"There was, and he was extremely powerful, so powerful the kingdom struggled to stop him regardless of what we used." Whit motioned to the pictures on the wall of different battles and powers tried during that dark time —powers that faded from faekind after the war including invoking Nyx's darkness. Laurel shivered as if from a bad memory. Cyrus shifted his weight. Whit pointed to a particularly dark scene with many fae and unicorn depicted as dead. It showed a fae victory but at great cost. "The king did favor your mother. She could have married him and lived out her days as the queen, but she was at her best on the battlefield."

Mother could have never fought in a battle and lived out her days in the palace I'd slept in last night. But that palace might not have stood if she hadn't fought. By the accounts here, the kingdom would have been lost. She chose the right side of history. My heart ached for her sacrifice, but I understood her choice.

Whit moved on to the next picture. "This painting is—"

I gasped and ran my fingers over the paint on the canvas. Incredible. It depicted a stunning show of the full power Mother had. She must have held so much back during her time in our kingdom. I recalled glimpses of her magic she kept hidden from most. She'd been a caged bird for my life...for the lives of the realm. Mother looked so much younger in the picture, even by fae standards. "She looks like me in this painting."

Whit's mouth turned down. "The abilities you saw from her, as great as they were, only accounted for a small portion of what she had in her. When the prison kingdom was created, the majority of her goddess-given strength was filtered into the glamour and magic to maintain the power of it."

I cast my eyes down to the floor, unable to look at any of them. "Our home was a prison."

That was why I only saw rare moments of power from Mother. Sadness stabbed me in the chest. Despair suffocated me. My heart shattered as the world I knew crumbled. The life I believed to be mine never existed.

Laurel's boots came toe-to-toe with mine. He lifted my chin, forcing me to meet his gaze. "Focus on my voice. I know you feel like you are about to break into two, but I'm not going to let that happen. Not to you. Not here."

Someone grasped my hand, and I glanced to see it was Cyrus's fingers intertwined with mine. I squeezed his fingers so tightly that my knuckles turned white. He didn't let go.

Laurel cradled my face in his hands. "Your mother's sacrifice was a gift to the entire kingdom, and she loved you so fiercely she was determined to get you and your sister out."

Some of the devastation loosened, and I could focus again. "So why didn't she?"

Laurel stepped to my side, taking my other hand. Whit moved back into my view. "When she became sick, she was in the process of arranging it. Then, we lost communication with her. She loved you and your sister so much, and she wanted you to be free of that prison and free of your father."

"Why had she waited that long? And why wouldn't my father need to be freed with us?" I asked. My strength returning, I loosened my grip on Cyrus and Laurel.

"She—" Laurel's voice cracked. He cleared his throat

and tried again. "She wanted to make sure you were old enough to help look after your sister. She understood how strange this world would seem to you both. It was important to her that you had each other."

"Because she couldn't leave. Even if she got us out, she had to stay. What about Father?"

Whit traced a finger along a painting and pointed to the figure leading the vampire opposite the fae in a particularly brutal battle scene. "He is her," Whit's said, his voice full of sadness. "I'm sorry to be the one to show you this."

"That can't be," I said, swaying and catching myself on Laurel's arm. Nausea soured my stomach and rose to the top of my throat. *It can't be true.* I stumbled, but Laurel steadied me.

"If I could take it all away, Gemma, I would." The devastation in his voice matched my insides. "The magic maintaining the space was hers. If she were to leave, the intricately woven magic and glamour would collapse. It was all designed to keep on prisoner in place—a traitor to faekind. Your father."

Instead of whisking me away, which was how I'd been treated when my mother's death came up in my home, Laurel gave the straight answer I deserved. It meant something to me—that he knew I was strong enough to handle the truth. My mind flashed to the inscription on Mother's statue.

"Chosen by Nyx..." I whispered.

"Yes."

Reality sharpened my focus on the information I'd

received. "Then why are they not down now? Why didn't they collapse after she died?"

Whit pointed to a portrait of Nyx and her children. Mother wasn't pictured there, but he traced an invisible line from Nyx to one of the goddesses. "The elders believe that because Daphina was gifted her magic directly from Nyx, only her descendants can create the same type of realm within a realm. This would be similar to how it is believed Nyx gifted her own children."

"But I'm here..." My voice went up an octave, matching my realization. "So, it's all on my sister. I have to get back to Ari. She can't die the same death my mother did."

I twisted away from them, needing to run but not having anywhere to go.

A familiar warmth slid down the bond. *Gemma, you need to calm down. There is more to it.*

Laurel grabbed my wrist in a loose hold. "You can't help her, Gemma. Or rather she doesn't need your help."

"What do you mean? You saw what it did to my mother." I yanked on his arm, but his grip held firm, though not too tight.

"Let her go, Laurel," Cyrus said, his voice low...too low. Then, down our bond came a soft soothing caress. *Relax and let him explain.*

I stopped struggling, and Laurel released my arm.

"Just listen for a minute before you go storming off." He ran his hand through his hair and focused on me again. "While Daphina was gifted by Nyx, Arianna's gift is something more. She hasn't discovered the true nature of it yet, and it might be some time before she does. Your mother was incredibly powerful, but your sister is even more so. We need to keep that truth from your father."

His desperation radiated off of him, so much so it permeated my emotions. "What would happen if my father found out?"

"He could give the vampires access to our kingdom again. It would be like the war never ended, only we have fewer of our allies to fight alongside us." Laurel shot a quick, almost apologetic glance at Cyrus.

Everything he said, as hard as it was to hear, made sense. I wanted to crumple where I stood, but I hardened myself against the pain. Whit had shown me the history, and nothing Laurel said contradicted it. "How do you know this for sure?"

"We've been sending people in for years under the guise of emissaries from other lands. Daphina wove it into the very fabric of the glamour so that we could move in and out without being detected."

"But how do you know of her power?"

Cyrus cleared his throat. Laurel looked relieved my bonded took the lead on this part. "My twin is your sister's bonded. He has long sensed her power."

Disbelief shook me. Ari would feel so betrayed. "Marius has been spying on my sister despite his sworn bond?"

Cyrus shook his head. "Only to figure out how to extract you both and leave the barrier intact."

He'd known. All this time. My bonded, instead of trusting me, worked behind my back on a plan with his brother and fae from this kingdom. I balled my fists.

Laurel and Whit took a step away. Rage built at the base of my spine and traveled up to my neck. I threw my arm out and punched at Cyrus. He caught it.

I burned my gaze into him, wishing I had fire magic like my sister. For his part, my bonded didn't squirm. To his credit, Cyrus met my gaze with the intensity of his own.

Laurel cleared his throat, but I ignored him.

"Stop," Cyrus said, his voice firm but gentle. "The goal was always to get you both out safely. You just had to run into the woods yesterday."

Was it only yesterday? That realization knocked the wind out of me. I rolled my shoulders to loosen the tension. I needed that reminder because I felt as if I'd known Laurel my entire life.

"So, it's my fault?" I jerked my arm free of his hand.

Cyrus pulled me into a hug, not letting me spiral any further. I melded to him, but it felt like something was missing. I ignored the urge to invite Laurel to wrap himself around my back. Although it was appealing as fuck, none of us needed the drama that sandwich would cause...and I wasn't sure it wouldn't end with Laurel getting a black eye from a unicorn.

CHAPTER 10

RED

GEMMA

Back in the lobby, I thanked Whit for all he'd shared with me today. He wore a weary expression on his face, and I could tell the day had likely taken as much of a toll on him as it had me. Inside, I was a mix of emotions. Cyrus and Laurel stayed close, and their presence kept me going to hear all the details. I waited at the door between Cyrus and Laurel. They'd both shadowed me the rest of the tour like I was so fragile. Normally, overprotectiveness annoyed me, but it comforted me from them, albeit in a bit of a smothering sort of way.

As hard as it was to not run out the door and back to Ari, I stayed and listened to every piece of the history Whit shared. The personal stories he recounted of times with my mother were the ones that touched me the most. He saw a side of her I never got to see...the warrior side. She was fierce, and I understood why Ari and I both were so passionate and confident in our ventures. As devastating as it was to hear, I believed the history I'd been shown.

The childhood Ari and I had was real. Our mother's love was real. The hardest part to reconcile was that we were in a prison because of my father's choices. The other side of our parentage left me conflicted. I wasn't even sure I wanted my sister to know who Father really was. Drew would be too young to even understand for years, but Ari was old enough. She deserved to know the truth as much as I did. But was it a burden I had to give her? Father, at least the persona Mother had created for him, referred to us as rambunctious and headstrong many times during our childhood. He never discouraged us though, and that was hard to reconcile with the evil I'd seen in the museum records. *Did my sister need to know those details?* I mulled the question over in my head. *Ari did need these same answers, but I'd have to be careful with the explanation.* Her magic's unpredictability tended to increase with her emotions, but I wouldn't keep the truth from her.

A smaller, bright red car pulled up in front of the museum. Armstrong pulled up in the car we arrived in right behind. He hurried toward the red car. A raven-haired woman wearing dark spectacles climbed out. As soon as she removed them, I knew who she was, and my stomach sank all the way to hell. *Merrick.*

Laurel stiffened like a statue next to me. *Shouldn't he be happy to see the woman he is in love with?* I inched closer to Cyrus, and he rested a hand on my back. The warm touch comforted my nerves.

She wore black boots and pants, and a pale blue sweater. Large diamond earrings dripped from her ears. She was striking, but her aura was red like her lips and the car she drove. Everything about her was meant to draw attention.

Armstrong opened the door for her, and the young man behind the front desk greeted Merrick with a hug.

"Hello, Quinn," she said, embracing the younger fae. She seemed genuinely happy to see him. Her eyes narrowed slightly as she took me in, but her lips, red like her car, turned up as she raked her gaze over Cyrus. I shifted and Cyrus slid his arm around my waist and squeezed—not enough to stop me but more as a warning. Being closer to him made me feel safe. Curious to see Laurel's reaction to Merrick, I paused and observed how their exchange unfolded.

She turned her smile to him. "I didn't realize you would be here today or that the palace was entertaining guests."

Laurel cleared his throat. "Let me introduce you to Princess Gemma and her bonded, Cyrus."

A smirk played at Merrick's lips as she contained it. "Princess of where?"

The condescension in her tone was clear, and I straightened my back, extending my hand. "I'm the daughter of General Daphina, savior of the kingdom and chosen by Nyx."

Her smirk turned down, and I took way too much satisfaction in how I'd won that round. People like Merrick were rarely surprised and were always looking a step ahead to gain the upper hand. She would unleash some wrath on me. It was only a matter of time, but I suspected she didn't want to do it directly in front of

Laurel—too afraid she'd destroy the image she'd crafted for him.

She looked at Laurel, and so did I. He was smiling at me as if pleased by my retort. That would no doubt be a challenge for Merrick.

Merrick took my hand. "I'm Merrick. Laurel's betrothed."

Even though he'd made me a priority today, she was his chosen person and wanted to make sure I understood her claim. I'd lost the upper hand...if I'd ever had it.

Laurel coughed like he'd swallowed wrong. "Merrick, we are not engaged."

She sighed, rolling her eyes, and placing her arm on his shoulder. "Why do you play like that, darling?" She looked at me and lifted a shoulder. "Men. He acts as if our marriage hasn't been planned for decades."

Decades...I'd only lived two and a half of those. They'd known each other longer than my lifetime.

"What are you doing here, Merrick?" Laurel asked, shifting away from her.

"I came to pick up Quinn."

"So, you didn't know we were here?"

I looked at Quinn, who was fidgeting, and his avoidance told me everything I needed to know as to how Merrick was here. She was the kind who would manipulate and hurt to get what she wanted, and if that was the type of woman Laurel wanted, that woman wouldn't be me.

"Why don't Cyrus and I head back, and you can catch up with your fiancée?"

"That won't be necessary," Laurel said. "Merrick's car only holds two people, so there wouldn't be room for me and Quinn."

"True." She smiled. "What time will the welcome celebration be for your guests?"

"We're not going to overwhelm our guests with something like that."

A ball would be a good distraction with the movement making good cover for an escape, but not being on display for the nobles of the kingdom was a relief.

"We must," Merrick said, a pout on her face. "I'll reach out to my staff and have them coordinate with yours. Eight o'clock should be good, right?"

She really didn't give up. I suspected she didn't hear no very often, but I'd trade my wind magic for Laurel to deny her request again.

Laurel's face sagged. "Fine, but make it nine."

My wind magic was safe. A breeze skated over my skin like an emphasis on my stupidity.

Merrick kissed his cheek and clapped her hands together. She gave me a once-over and sneered. "I hope you brought your best party clothes."

I smiled back. I'd spied a couple of beautiful, banquet-appropriate dresses in the closet. My stomach sank. Were those her clothes in the closet? *Is that why she sneered at me?* I scooted deeper into Cyrus's protective arm as he guided me to the car.

I slid to the middle of the seat, and Cyrus sat next to me. I was grateful for him and even more grateful to be away from Merrick. The air lightened without her nearby.

Laurel's shoulder brushed against mine. "Will you be disappointed if we postpone your driving lesson?"

"Red is your color," I said, turning my attention to the front. The driving lesson was unnecessary since I'd made up my mind to leave first thing in the morning. My sister needed me, and her friend, Valentina, would talk to my ladies. Ari would start suspecting something was wrong, and if she went to Father, neither one of us would get out of the castle without a slew of guards again.

"What?" Laurel asked, confused.

Cyrus put his elbow on the door near the bottom of the window, placing his hand beside his mouth. "She's talking about the red lip prints on your face."

Laurel wiped at the marks and smeared them. Armstrong handed him a white handkerchief. "Thanks."

For someone in love, he didn't seem to want to be around her. Or maybe it was a game between them. Or maybe the marriage was arranged as Merrick insinuated. Or maybe I was overthinking because I was attracted to this infuriating man. "I think you will need soap and water to get that off."

He studied the white cloth, now a shade of pink. "Is it still there?"

"More of it is on your face than the handkerchief."

"Goddesses and gods, what do you women use on your lips?"

"Women?" My brow arched in that way I couldn't control when I was mad. "Not all of us wear what she had on but maybe ask your future wife that question."

His mouth fell open. He closed it and it fell open again, but no sound came out.

The car circled into the open space in front of the door to the palace. I pushed Cyrus against the door.

"Hmmph." He pulled the handle and stumbled out before turning to hold his hand out for me. "In a hurry?"

"I need to be alone." I walked past him and in through the door the guard held open.

CHAPTER II

SANDWICHES

LAUREL

A s cute as it was to see her jealous and as much as that made me feel worthy of her, I couldn't let her keep wandering around looking for the wing of the palace with our suites. I mean, I could, but I suspected that would only serve to stoke the fire of anger ready to erupt from her.

"Our rooms are this way if that's where you were going." I gestured to the right hallway.

Gemma cut her eyes at me and leveled a vicious look that had me stepping back from her, and I didn't back down from anyone—not even my brother with all his power.

"Don't show fear," Cyrus whispered next to me.

She turned her gaze toward him. "Since you are friends with him now, you can stay in his room."

Cyrus smirked. "Unicorns don't answer to fae."

He teased her, but her face turned bright red. I took a

giant step away from him, sure she was about to obliterate the unicorn where he stood. Instead, she spun on her heels and took fast, clipped steps toward her suite.

She needed time to cool down, and I was curious about the unicorn still standing there. My stomach growled.

"Hungry?" I asked Cyrus.

"I could eat," he said.

"Let's see what's in the kitchen." I waved the guards off and led the way.

"Do you eat sandwiches?"

"Vegetarian."

I nodded. Cyrus's faelike form was solid, and he had been in it for an extended period of time. I'd never seen a unicorn take human form without the shimmer of glamour around them. "How do you hold it so long?"

He cocked an eyebrow at me. The ambiguity and randomness of the question hit me square in the gut.

My face heated. "The glamour."

"Oh." He lifted a shoulder. "We all have our gifts—unicorn and fae."

I set the loaf of bread on the cutting board and sliced four equal slices. "I'm not with Merrick. I haven't been for a long time."

"Why are you telling me?"

"You're her guardian." I opened the refrigerator and pulled ingredients, stacking them in my arms. There was a freshly made batch of my favorite green dressing, and I found some spinach, cucumber, avocado, and feta cheese.

After a longing look at the sliced meat the cook had left for my regular visits, I closed the door.

"Gemma is her own person. She wouldn't like us talking about her."

He was right. She wouldn't want anyone to talk about her or speak for her.

"Then let's talk about you instead." I worked on stacking the ingredients on the bread.

Cyrus crossed his arms over his chest. Whether fae or unicorn in human form, there weren't many who could compare. "She likes you." His voice sounded a little defeated.

That little bit he gave away told me my suspicions were right. He cared more for her than the unicorn bond. An image of the three of us flashed through my mind, and my dick twitched. I let out a breath to release some of the tension. Fae loved freely, and while my experiences included multiple fae, I'd never been with a unicorn.

"I'm attracted to her." I liked her more than I wanted to admit, but I wanted to get to know him too.

"Good. Don't fuck it up. Anything else you want to know? Ask her."

Which was the mature thing to do as a two hundred-and-twenty-year-old fae, but a peek inside her thoughts, like he had, would be helpful. I slid the plate with his sandwich over to him. He took a bite.

"We don't bond with unicorns here anymore."

He nodded as he chewed. Was now the right time to ask about the attraction I had for him? It only seemed to be growing, and if it was some vibe from their link, he would know.

"I feel a connection with Gemma. Is the bond why I feel a similar, fainter one to you?"

Cyrus stopped chewing. An unreadable expression crossed his face before it returned to neutral. I could have sworn I saw some curiosity prior to him masking it. He swallowed.

I took a large bite of my sandwich to keep from filling the silence with word vomit.

His face scrunched up in a dismissive look. "Likely. You haven't been around true bonded in two hundred years, and you are a healer—or doctor, as you call the profession now. I suspect you have strong empath skills to have selected that profession."

"Yes, I do."

"It used to be quite common for empaths to sense bonds between fae and unicorn or mates or similar."

"I hadn't thought of that. Thank you for the explanation." I took a huge bite of my sandwich, trying to eat the rest in a hurry. I wanted nothing more than to get out of the awkward situation I'd created. *Goddesses and gods, save me.*

"If you hurt Gemma, I'll spear you with my horn." A feral grin spread across his face.

I choked on my food. He walked around the counter and patted my back. I got the food down and turned to him. "I'm fine."

His face was close to mine, and a little kernel of desire flickered in my cock.

The door swung open. Cyrus jerked his head toward the opening. I bit back a laugh. The cook looked at me and the mess I'd made.

She shook her head and smiled. It wasn't the first time she'd caught me in the kitchen with someone...or a few someones. At least all parties were clothed when she walked in on me this time.

CHAPTER 12
THE GOWN
ARC COPY

I sat on the edge of the bathtub while it filled. There had been two ladies' maids in the room when I returned. Before I kicked her out of the bathing chamber, one of them suggested I add bubbles to my bath to relax. She left me to go pick out some options for the evening event. I'd looked forward to parties at my home, but I dreaded seeing Merrick again. Moreover, I didn't want to see Laurel with her or have this party to rub my face in their relationship, which was what I was sure she wanted to do. My plan was unchanged—I'd leave tomorrow morning. I just needed to focus on getting through this stupid banquet.

The bubbles reached the rim of the tub, and I found the knob to turn the water off. I ran my fingers through the fizz to test the water. Mother had been from here— used to baths with bubbles, probably drove cars, and might have lived in buildings so tall the roof couldn't be seen from the street. And so many people. I'd be lying to myself if I didn't acknowledge it felt normal to me—like home. My sister wasn't a fan of change. Even if Ari knew the truth, she wouldn't like it here. She was happy in our home, but I hadn't been in a while. What if the Fates had a hand in getting me here?

I slipped out of my clothes and into the warm water. The maid was right about it being relaxing. Tension evaporated from my muscles. The throbbing in my head eased, but the emotions and strain of the day weighed on my body. I needed to escape, but it wasn't from this kingdom. It was the knowledge that everything I'd known was a fabrication, and the kingdom I stumbled into yesterday with Laurel was reality.

Laurel...I wanted to hate him, but he'd only been kind and showed me the truth. The other truth I couldn't ignore was that I liked him, despite his...whatever Merrick was to him. He said they weren't engaged, and he seemed firm about it. I leaned against the back and rested my head on it, sinking further into the water. Skimming my hand over my belly, I found the sensitive nub that would give me the release I needed. I thought of Laurel as my fingers reached my most sensitive area. His smile took on a wicked turn as I thought of his lips moving down my body to where my fingers were. Fire burned through my skin. My pace quickened. I imagined him positioning me at the edge of the tub to get access and him thrusting in and out of me. My breath came in little rasps. He lifted me up and I wrapped my legs around his waist. Then, there was Cyrus, in his human form, at my back stroking me. His hand was down where Laurel and I were connected. Cyrus rubbed the head of his cock there. My arousal grew, and I moved my fingers faster.

A knock rapped at the door. I shattered in the tub and bit down on my hand to keep my cries to a minimum. I inhaled a few breaths, letting my climax subside.

"Yes?" I called.

"Not to rush you, ma'am, but we need to get started with your hair."

My orgasm wasn't cut short, but I would have preferred to ride out my fantasy a little longer. That left me frustrated. "I'll be out in a minute."

I'd just fantasized about my enemy and my bonded both fucking me. Was Laurel really my enemy? No matter who he was, I'd had the best orgasm ever, even with the interruption. Fantasizing hadn't been something I had done before, and I'd never been with two men—or a man and a unicorn. It excited me, but unicorns didn't hook up with fae and especially not with their bonded, so all that could ever be was a fantasy. Still, the moment in my little indulgence felt right to me. I finished washing quickly and climbed out of the tub. The robe hanging nearby fit perfectly. My reflection in the mirror caught my attention. I ran my finger over my pink cheeks. Would I blush like this if I had them both?

I loved Cyrus. He was my bonded, and I'd felt the change between us around the time I turned twenty and the allure grew over the last five years—at least on my part. I didn't know if he reciprocated the attraction. With Laurel, a magnetic pull drew me to him in a way I hadn't been with anyone else. Our little touches set electrical charges off in my body. *What is going on with me? I can't have either of them.* I loosed a breath and opened the door.

"I didn't catch your name earlier," I said. "Apologies for not asking."

She smiled. "No apology needed. I'm Sarah."

"Thank you for helping me, Sarah. I'm Gemma."

"Yes, ma'am."

"Please call me Gemma."

She inclined her head, and I was thankful she didn't curtsy. I abhorred that tradition in my...home. That home seemed fake now as if it never existed. My memories ached in a tainted reality. My sister and brother were still there and safe in the false reality as long as the magic held. I wouldn't ruin the only home they'd ever known. When I returned tomorrow, I wouldn't reveal any of this to them until the others came to extract us—whether that was a week or ten years from now. My chest twinged at the idea, and I wasn't sure if it was for not wanting to tell them or for the thought of being distanced from Laurel for years.

"If you'll sit at the dressing table, I can start with your hair."

"Thank you," I said, sitting on the padded stool in front of the table. There were brushes, hairpins, curling tools, and various hair items. I was capable of doing my own hair, but I had ladies with me at home who did my hair and dressed me, especially for special events.

"You know you don't have to keep thanking me. This is my job." She ran the brush through my hair. "Do you normally wear your hair up or down?"

"Usually up for an evening event, but I noticed that

doesn't appear to be how it is done here." The women I'd seen here didn't seem to have a set way to wear theirs, and I liked the freedom of styling it down versus the usual updo I wore at home.

"We could curl it into soft waves if you wear the red dress." Sarah tilted her head to where three gowns hung— a black sequined one, a shimmering champagne-colored dress with a full skirt, and a red one cut to skim the body. The dress was beautiful. Red wasn't a color I would normally wear. Ari's friend Valentina wore red a lot because it was their house color. Maybe it was time to do the unexpected. "Do you like it?"

"I do. Do women here wear dresses so... form-fitting?"

Her brows scrunched together. "That one is quite modest compared to many you will see."

I let out a breath, determined to embrace this experience because I would have to return to my sister and brother, and this would all be a dream. The dress was cut low. I'd be showing a lot of cleavage, but the drape from the cinched waist was like a waterfall. It wasn't like I'd have to look at anyone here for much longer. "The red gown it is."

CHAPTER 13
FIRST DANCE
GEMMA

A knock came from the door. I took one last look in the mirror and smoothed my hands over the dress. My breasts were pushed together to create a nearly obscene display of cleavage. My curves were accentuated in every way, and I'd never have been able to wear this gown at home. The choice not only made me feel pretty but empowered me.

I opened the door to see Laurel and Cyrus waiting for me. Laurel's eyes widened and his mouth fell open as if he was going to say something, but then he closed it.

Cyrus cleared his throat. "You look lovely, Gemma."

My cheeks heated, but I'd never felt more beautiful. Both men wore black suits. One of the ladies had called them tuxedos when she explained them to me. Cyrus had the shorter jacket version and Laurel the longer one she'd called a tailcoat.

"I was hoping you would choose that dress. I have the perfect necklace to wear with it," Laurel said, opening a velvet box. A diamond cluster necklace with marquise and pear-shaped diamonds set at various angles rested like a crown in the box. It resembled a flower with petals or leaves that kept going all the way around to the clasp.

"It's beautiful," I said, tracing my fingers around the edge of the necklace and skimming over the soft velvet.

"It was my mother's. I'll put it on you." He motioned for me to turn around.

I lifted my hair. "Are you sure you want me to wear it?"

"It belongs on someone who matches the fire of the gems." Laurel's fingers brushed my neck as he clasped the necklace. Goosebumps peppered my skin. The images of my fantasy with both of them invaded my mind.

"Shall we?" Laurel whispered against my ear.

My belly clenched. I pressed my free hand to my stomach and let my hair down. Laurel swept my curls back over my shoulder.

"You are perfection."

I turned around to Laurel's beaming expression, his cheeks glowing. A yearning look crossed Cyrus's face, and I'd never seen it before. With the two men so close and staring at me, it was like I stood there naked. My heart pounded. Both Cyrus and Laurel held their elbows out. All I could think of was how good they looked in my fantasy, but they were both more handsome and enticing waiting for me. My cheeks burned. I hastily looped my arms through each of theirs, and we headed down the hall.

The walk was silent for the most part save our footfalls. I was afraid to say anything. Maybe they were too. Music meandered around us, so I could tell we were getting closer. Aromas drifted around us—some sweet and some savory. I wondered how the entrance was done and why I hadn't asked about protocol. *Did I enter first as a guest or would Laurel be announced first?*

Two finely dressed men flanked the doors and opened them as we approached. I looked to Laurel for an indication of what to do, but he strolled forward without a pause. He didn't slow down as we crossed the threshold to a full ballroom. The music kept playing and didn't stop for us. Then men and women turned in our direction, and I wasn't sure what was happening. This wasn't the custom I was used to. They stared like we were an art piece, and I'd never felt more uncomfortable in my life. My palms were sweaty, and it reminded me of my coronation as the crown princess at fifteen. The attention asphyxiated me. I regretted the dress with so many eyes on me.

"Are they going to bow or something? Why are they all staring?" I asked Laurel.

"I believe they are wondering how I got so lucky as to have the most beautiful woman in the room on my arm, who happens to be General Daphina's daughter."

Oh, that's it. Not the dress. Relief loosened the tension in my shoulders. I looked like my mother...a lot, so they were probably trying to figure it out unless they were informed already. Cyrus stiffened beside me, and his protective anger vibrated off him.

"It's fine, big guy. No unicorn fists." Crude gestures wouldn't win any friends.

"Two of my least favorite phrases," Cyrus said in an annoyed tone.

"Please continue as you were," Laurel said in a loud, commanding voice over the music. The music halted, then resumed in a light happy tune I didn't know. Everyone went back to talking amongst their groups. The casual acceptance blew me away. Everything at home, that word seemed less and less normal to describe where I'd come from, was more formal. Paired entries to a gala would have been announced in order of court rank, and I no longer had that. When I returned to Ari and Drew, I'd have to pretend to be the crown princess again. Because that was all it had been—make-believe. How would I fall back into that role knowing what I learned? For Ari and Drew's sake, that was how.

"That was..."

"Normal here," Laurel finished and led us from the most crowded area to a table that was positioned away from the others. No dais like I was used to, but the regalia denoted the table of honor. "They will gawk unless you call them out. That's why I had all phones confiscated as they arrived. I didn't want any pictures you didn't approve ending up on the gossip sites. I'm sure there are some from our outings earlier already."

"Gossip sites?"

"Similar to the news you saw on the TV."

The pictures were like portraits. Laurel had shown me how to take them from his pocket-sized phone. He'd taken a couple of me and then we took something together he called a selfie. It was fun, but it was intimate too. I wouldn't want random pictures from these people being shared like on those TV shows. "There were stories about you. Is that what you mean?"

"Yes, some of the gossip shows will say anything to get viewers to watch."

"You mean tell lies?"

He pulled a padded chair out for me. The velvet fabric was blue and plush and the seat so large it could be a throne. Every chair at the table was the same though...no throne in the room. "More like bending the truth in a salacious way."

Cyrus was fuming as he took the chair on the other side of me. His silence was unusual, and I kept scanning over to him to make sure he wasn't about to do something we'd all regret.

Laurel dropped into the chair next to me and draped his arm over the back of mine. I immediately felt safer. He leaned in close to me. "That dress was meant for turns across the ballroom. We could hit the dance floor."

"Hit the floor?" I asked, curious why a partygoer would strike the floor.

Laurel gave me an easy smile. "It means dancing."

"No one is dancing," Cyrus said looking around me at Laurel.

What's up with you? I sent to my bonded.

Nothing. Why?

You seem a bit on edge.

I'm fine.

He didn't seem fine. He sounded agitated, even in our communication down the bond.

You do look beautiful.

I smiled. *Thank you.*

"Is your brother joining us?" I asked, wondering if the cold storm of a man would partake in the festivities.

"He will be. Dinner will be served when he arrives. Are you hungry?"

Waitstaff stopped at our table with trays of cocktails and hors d'oeuvres. I recognized most, like the stuffed dates and stuffed mushrooms, but the flaky, buttery cheese cookie was the selection that had my mouth watering. I took two of those. Another one the waiter called a brussels sprout with a savory jam. It tasted bitter and reminded me of eating dirt as a child. I left it on a napkin. Laurel casually motioned the servers away, and they mingled through the crowd.

"A little food would be good."

His brows bunched together. "You didn't eat a midday meal."

My cheeks burned. "I took a bath. I wasn't hungry."

"Don't skip any more meals. You need your strength." He studied me, and the serious set of his kind face said there was something more in his words than just my nourishment.

I almost asked what I needed my strength for, but I was afraid of the answer. The wine scent wafted up around me, and I grabbed the glass, taking a big swig. The fruity liquid burned down my throat and warmed my belly. I set the glass down and my arm brushed against Cyrus's. I looked up into his gaze and saw concern that melted into liquid heat. My insides turned molten in response.

The room went silent. My chest felt heavy, making it hard to breathe. Were the high fae born of noble houses who revered my mother about to reject me? Kick me out of their ball? I straightened my back as I'd been trained. *Never let anyone at court see your weakness.* Lessons from my youth played back in my head. If the highborn here wanted me gone, would I be able to return home? I glanced around the space, finding Rainier standing at the entrance. My shoulders relaxed a little. He was dressed in a tuxedo similar to Laurel's, but he had a sash and pin in the kingdom's blue and silver colors. The room bowed and curtseyed for him, but it was far less formal than my experiences at home. I moved to rise, and Laurel slid his arm around my shoulder at the same time Cyrus placed a hand on my knee.

"You bend your knee for no one." Laurel's breath brushed against my ear. My eyelids fluttered as goosebumps rose down my arm. "Except me."

My core clenched so tightly I drew in a breath.

Cyrus made a noise close to a growl. A twinge of something akin to desire came through the bond. I swallowed the need the feeling stirred in me and focused on the dark-haired figure approaching us dressed in one of the tuxedos like Laurel wore.

Rainier approached our table in a deliberate saunter. "Gemma, I don't have a date this evening, and I'd be honored if you would be my first dance."

In my former home, it was traditional for the honored guest to open a party with the first dance, so I assumed it was the custom here. The only problem was neither Laurel nor Cyrus had eased their hold on me.

"Yes, I'm feeling a little..."

"Smothered?" Rain offered with a smile.

"Precisely."

Cyrus extracted his hand from my knee, but Laurel didn't move. I didn't want to break the connection, but I couldn't catch my breath. If I didn't get a break from Laurel and Cyrus, I might combust in front of the watchful eyes of the highest-ranking fae in this kingdom.

Laurel's lips brushed my earlobe. "He gets your first dance, but I get your last. No one else but me."

I met his gaze and saw a promise, not a threat, looking back at me. Cyrus made another low rumble like a growl and broke my trance with Laurel. He released me, and I rose from the chair.

Rainier met me at the end of the table with his hand extended. I slipped mine in his. "You have quite the blush on your face," he said as he nodded to the musicians. A melody I wasn't familiar with began to fill the vast space of the ballroom.

"It's a little warm in here."

He chuckled and led me through the steps. "You look lovely, Gemma."

"Thank you," I said as he spun me around. "Whoever picked out my wardrobe selected well." Rainier was a good dancer, and I wondered if Laurel would be as well. A striking figure in the doorway caught my attention. Merrick.

My stomach sank. A part of me hoped she'd dropped

dead between earlier when we met earlier and the start of the ball. She glanced in my direction and cast her eyes the other way. I followed her gaze straight to Laurel. She gave a smile to others as she made her way across to Laurel.

My neck tensed, but I tempered my features to a practiced neutral. *He's not mine, no matter how much I like him.*

"Relax. It's not what you think."

"What?" I looked back at Rainier.

"He's not into her. Maybe when we were younger, and before she was...not who she is today, he might have loved her. But he doesn't anymore."

He hadn't fully earned my trust, but I believed him on the topic of Merrick. "How does he feel about you telling me that?"

"My brother would probably be happy I did since I embarrassed him last night." Rainier's voice was softer when he said that as if he was truly remorseful. He meant the hallway conversation I stumbled upon while in a too-sheer nightgown. Heat flushed my cheeks. Had I misjudged them both?

"Neither of you is what I expected. Nor is your kingdom."

"This is your kingdom too, Gemma. Your mother made this kingdom what it is today. It wouldn't even exist..." His voice thickened. "I think she would be happy and grateful to see you become a leader here."

His words touched me. He'd let down a piece of the sarcastic wall for me...for the daughter of the great general he remembered, and that meant something to me. Acceptance. "Thank you, Prince Rainier."

"Please, call me Rain. My brother would never let me live it down if he heard you call me Prince Rainier."

I laughed.

"He likes you, Gemma. More than I remember seeing him like anyone in decades. Don't break his heart."

I was about to ask him what made him think that when Merrick with her red lips danced so close to us that I couldn't without her hearing. Then I noted her partner. Laurel.

The look on his face was stressed, and I didn't take pleasure in seeing him that way. Rainier spun me and proclaimed, "Switch."

"Uh..." Merrick sneered at me before spinning into Rain's arms.

Laurel rested one hand on my waist and grasped my fingers with the other. I mouthed a quick thank you to Rainier, then Laurel guided our steps until we were a good distance away from his brother and his...whatever the fuck she was.

PART TWO

TEARS

From the field notebook of Albert in his final year at university. This diary was recovered from his dwelling when the insurrection started and is currently held in secret by the curator of the War Museum.

The results of my DNA test arrived today. My mother and father lied to me about my birth. I am King Veran's son. The nosferatu spoke the truth. While the circumstances are not clear, neither of the fae who raised me are my biological parents. King Veran will pay for discarding me like trash. I will gradually take his throne by robbing him of enough of his sanity to lose the trust of his people

but leaving him enough he will see his kingdom
fall to me.

CHAPTER 14

STAY
LAUREL

My brother didn't often use his position to benefit me, but I was thankful he did tonight. There was no other woman in this room I wanted to touch except Gemma.

"I hope Rain didn't say anything offensive. He's not known for being gentle with his words." I studied her fine features. Her hazel eyes were greener in this light, and her nose turned up ever so slightly at the end. She was as beautiful as she was strong, and I didn't want to let her go. I would if she wanted to return home, but I hoped she'd listen to reason and stay.

"He was actually quite the gentleman."

My mouth started to slide open, and I closed it quickly, setting my features to neutral. "Was he now?"

"We talked about you."

My heart pounded, and my cheeks warmed like the sun blistered them. "Me?"

"Are you sure there isn't anything between you and

Merrick?" Gemma cocked an eyebrow up as if daring me to spill my story. I liked her a little jealous. It told me she might feel the same way I did.

"Did he say there was? I'll—"

She tightened her grip on mine. "He didn't suggest there was. I'm asking for me."

Excited by her strength, my breath quickened. The room had too many people, and I wanted her to myself. "Would you like to get out of here? Go somewhere we can talk?"

She shivered in my arms. "Yes, I'd like to go somewhere where there are not so many eyes staring at me."

I knew that feeling well. There were always eyes on me —inside the palace or outside. It didn't matter. I glanced at Cyrus, who looked like he was ready to explode. His eyes were narrowed on us, and his arms were crossed. He looked sexy when he was mad. "Do you want to tell him to come along?"

"Keep dancing and give me a second." Her eyes went distant, but she kept time with the music. Seeing her communicate with him down the bond was impressive. I'd love to be in the middle of their discussion—to hear those thoughts firsthand. "He'll trail behind us. We can go."

A moment alone with Gemma had blood pumping to my lower extremities, and I thought of pigs wallowing in mud to keep myself in check. She slipped her arm into the crook of mine. I tucked it close to my body and led her out the door toward one of the research labs. No one would be at my personal lab tonight. I glanced over my shoulder to see Cyrus a good distance behind us. Why was the thought of him joining us so appealing? *Focus, Laurel.* He might be interested in what I was about to show her.

"What area is this? I don't remember seeing it when you gave me the tour."

"This is our research wing. There's a training facility adjacent to it as well. The spaces are all reinforced to protect the rest of the palace in case there is an incident."

The lights in the hallway flicked on as I navigated us past other rooms to the door I wanted. I put my hand on the panel to my office and lab. The door opened in front of her. My research here might be the key to swaying her to stay, but either way, she needed to know what we were doing. "Cyrus, you may want to come in too."

Gemma gave me an unreadable look. "Are you a healer, Laurel?"

"Our term here is doctor. We do have some that still practice as healers, but what I do is considered a doctor." I led Gemma inside and was pleased when Cyrus followed.

Cyrus closed the door and leaned against it. Even brooding, the unicorn was hot. I wondered for not the first time why Gemma hadn't taken him to bed and had to remind myself it was not an accepted practice in the world she grew up in.

I took Gemma's hand in mine and let the charge tickle my palm. "This is what I wanted to show you."

She studied the whiteboard with some of my research on it I positioned her in front of. "In our kingdom, magic and technology are intertwined. One is used where the other is weak and vice versa."

"Impressive," she said, considering the formulas and notes. I hadn't expected her to understand the complex diagrams and empirical data, but her gaze darted over every inch of it. She was everything I'd wished for—brains, beauty, strength, and a desire to help others. The latter was something we could share if she would accept a future with me. I hoped to see her gaze move over my body, consuming it the same way she did this information.

"What is this one here that is reducing?"

Cyrus joined us at the board. He grimaced harder as he took in each line. His posture stiffened, and I knew he already understood. "That is the rate the magic in our world is reducing."

Her eyes widened. "Why is that happening?"

"Because my kind is dying off." Cyrus let out a long sigh.

She turned to Cyrus, concern etched in her features. "What do you mean?"

"Since the war and even before, but the war made it worse, unicorns have not been able to reproduce. How many have you seen born in your lifetime?"

"One," she said. I could almost see her mind working out a solution. "But we were told that was normal. That unicorns weren't born without a purpose, so it meant things were right in our lands."

Cyrus's face was drawn, and his shoulders rose with tension. "But unicorns were always born. Yes, each of us has a purpose for our place, but we've never been in a position where there are fewer born than have left us."

Gemma's forehead bunched with concern. "What does it mean?"

"I've been working with my brother's bonded. She's not as forthcoming, but I share all my data with her."

Cyrus huffed. "The answer you are looking for, Gemma, is that magic will cease to exist in this world if we continue on this path."

I'd have told her a bit more gently than the way he did, but he spoke the truth. He knew Gemma and understood her better than me, but I wanted to change the outcome. To do that, I needed more help in the lab.

"What are you doing about it?" She fisted her hands in her dress as she shifted her gaze between me and Cyrus.

"We're trying to understand why it's happening. If we understood the root cause, then we might be able to fix it."

Cyrus crossed his arms over his chest but offered nothing, similar to what Rain's unicorn paring, Casimir, did. She'd take all the information I'd give, but she didn't offer much in return.

"Is it a disease?"

I waited to see if Cyrus would offer any explanation, but either he didn't know, or he wouldn't share.

"We don't know yet," I said.

"I'd like to help. What can I do? There must be something." The desperation in her voice caused my chest to tighten. She grasped the gravity of the situation.

"Stay," I said and studied her face.

Recognition of what I was asking flicked through her features. Not just for her to stay here and help with research but to stay for me. Rain was right. I wasn't just falling for Gemma. I'd already fallen for her. It was like the Fates themselves were pushing me to her—not that I needed that big a push. She was the smartest, sexiest-without-even-trying, beautiful fae I'd ever seen.

Gemma glanced at Cyrus. They must have communicated down their bond, and I wanted to crawl inside their connection to hear them. She rested one hand on his cheek, and he nestled into her touch. She touched my cheek with her other hand and met my gaze. My heart thundered with need. I brushed my lips against her palm.

"I can only stay if Cyrus will. My bonded must have a role here as well."

Cyrus stepped back. Taking her fingers in his, he patted the back of her hand with his. I imagined a silent exchange happening down their bond and wondered what it would be like to be invited into their sacred space.

I expected her to ask for Cyrus to stay, but what surprised me was I wanted him to stay too. For the first time in my two centuries, I wished I could command a unicorn. "Unicorns don't answer to fae. He's free to do as he pleases."

"Maybe you two should talk alone," Cyrus said, heading to the door. "I'm going to meet with Casimir."

"You know Rain's bonded?" I asked, realizing the ignorance of my statement after it was out of my mouth. She was old and so was he.

"Yes, my entire life," Cyrus said, and the door closed behind him.

Gemma watched the door, and I wondered if she wanted to follow Cyrus. Taking her to my room seemed forward, but I wasn't ready to stop talking with her. If she'd join me, I wanted more time with her. "Would you be agreeable to retiring to my rooms for a private chat?"

"It's not private here?" she challenged.

"It is, but I thought we might be more comfortable talking if we were sitting on my couch versus this hard desk." I smiled and knocked on the wood.

She blushed, and I loved how I affected her. The rosy color of her cheeks went straight to my dick, but that wasn't what I wanted to show her. I wanted to talk to her about what life would be like here if she stayed. Most importantly, she wouldn't be able to visit her sister or brother, which was the one thing I thought might be the deal-breaker.

CHAPTER 15

SHOW ME

GEMMA

L aurel handed me one of the mugs of coffee he made with the noisy machine on the counter. His jacket discarded over a chair, he sat on the opposite end of the light blue sofa and faced me. Everything in me wanted him closer, but my dress created space around me like a barrier. I had all night. It nearly drove me into a rage when Merrick was touching him, and it was immature of me. He'd asked me here to talk, and that was what we were going to do.

I sipped the coffee, and it was more flavorful than what we had back home. "Is there nutmeg in this?"

He smiled, and it lit up the room. "I hope you like it."

"I do," I said. "But I don't think you asked me here to discuss coffee flavors."

His throat bobbed, and I realized he was nervous. He was always so polished. What was he about to say that would have him flustered?

"I'd planned to ease into the conversation, but one

thing I've learned with you is that you don't appreciate added fluff to news."

"Fluff?" I arched a deliberate brow at him, amused by his approach. He was adorable in a situation he perceived as awkward. "No, I'm not a fan of fluff."

His shoulders relaxed a fraction. "If you choose to stay here, Gemma, you need to know what that means."

The thought of giving up my siblings, even temporarily, shredded my heart. Ari had Marius and Leana, Cyrus's stunning paired match, had taken an interest in Drew. They would be protected. If I were to be of any help in saving the unicorns and the ultimate survival of all of us, I could only do that from Laurel's kingdom. I set my cup on the coaster on the table. "So, no fluff then. Tell me what I'm getting into."

He shifted on the couch, his knee coming closer to mine. "You'll be giving up your old life in your father's prison kingdom. You will not be able to visit your friends or your sister and your brother."

"Do you mean ever?"

He pursed his lips and shook his head from side to side slowly.

"Exposing the path between the kingdoms puts them and us at risk." He anticipated my next question as if he knew me that well, or maybe I was just that readable. Laurel lifted a hand, but let it drop on the back of the couch. My stomach sank to the pits of hell. I'd expected not to be able to go back and forth frequently but to not visit them at all? The bodice of the gown, suddenly too tight, constricted my breathing. I wanted to rip it off to get air.

I thought of what my mother had risked to protect this kingdom and me and my sister. Mother wanted me to know this place, but I needed to understand everything to make my decision. Focusing my thoughts there, the tightness in my chest relaxed. "How? Explain it to me. I need all the facts."

He nodded. "The enemy your father aligned with— "

"The vampires...nosferatu."

"Yes, the vampires. They have been randomly testing our lines at the border. Apparently, they learned your father was alive. We'd led them to believe he was dead at the end of the war, but we think they have learned of the prison and are trying to locate it."

I wouldn't risk my family by being the one to expose the hidden path to our home. Strange. It didn't sit right with me calling it my home anymore, and I knew I'd not risk my brother and sister by returning. Unicorn protection was stronger than anything I could do. If I stayed, would Leana leave Drew to come be with Cyrus? Then what? Bringing my siblings here needed to be a priority.

But how did I know what Laurel said was true? He hadn't lied to me so far, and his aura was still warm like the sun. I'd let him explain. "Why after all this time?"

"A chance to restore Albert to power and restore the blood sources they enjoy most."

I wrapped my hand around my throat. "Ours?"

The set of his face hardened as if the thought alone

made him angry, and I empathized with that sentiment. "Yes, and the unicorns."

The thought of a vampire feeding on our enchanted friends soured my stomach. The image of them feeding on Cyrus painted my vision red with my rage. I wouldn't let that happen. Every bit of my magic would be made available to stop them. As my anger tempered, sadness crept into my chest at how few unicorns still walked the realm. "Even with their numbers dwindling?"

"They don't care about survival of the source as long as they get a taste."

I gagged and covered my mouth. "That's vile."

"That was almost what our world was to become before your mother led us to victory." He stared at me, and it felt as if he was assessing me. "Nothing is stopping you from leaving, Gemma, but if you return to the prison world, you might not be able to come back here. We have to stop revealing the passage until we figure out what to do with Albert." Laurel's expression was sadness and defeat and none deeper than in his eyes. Something else unsaid lay in the amber pools.

Every mention of my father's traitorous ways was a stab to the heart, as if it erased a part of me, but that wasn't the case. I wanted to make what he'd done wrong right in the realm. The choice was mine on what to do, and I'd made my decision. I'd made it the moment I'd learned what Mother had told me was real. "Laurel, my family means everything to me."

He nodded and played with one of the curls of my hair.

"And that is why I will stay and do whatever it takes,

even if that is a sacrifice like my mother's, to keep them safe. I give you my word as the daughter of General Daphina."

He raised his head and met my gaze, and I saw hope, but it looked like more than for the promise I'd just made. Tears pooled in his eyes as if sharing the details cost him something. Maybe a piece of his vulnerability because I felt closer to him.

I scooted toward him on the couch. He slipped his hands into my hair and curled them at the base of my neck. I leaned toward him and tilted my head, wanting and needing a taste of him. My heart pounded in my chest as the heat of his body warmed my skin.

His lips barely touched mine, but it was like setting fire to dry wood. My entire body ignited, and I pulled him closer until we tumbled backward on the couch. The bulk of the dress bunched up under my hips until his hard bulge pressed against my center. Still, I couldn't get him close enough. It wasn't possible. I wanted everything between us to disappear. I wanted to feel his skin against mine. I wanted him.

He kissed my cheek and dragged his lips along my jawline.

A small gasp fluttered out of my mouth. A tingle started in my stomach and spread out through my body.

He pushed up on his hands and studied me.

"Gemma." My name sounded like a prayer on his lips. "Are you sure about this?"

I pulled the thing around his neck loose—the tie—and

tossed it on the table. "I always know what I want, Laurel, and I want you."

He kissed the tip of my nose. "Then let's take this to my bedroom."

Laurel stood and scooped me up off the couch. I'd made a decision that would alter the course of my life, but my gut told me I'd chosen right. He kissed my forehead. "I've thought about this...a lot."

My center dampened at his words. I'd thought about it too. Of course, mine had included Cyrus, but that was a fantasy. This was reality, and I wanted Laurel more than I'd wanted anyone.

He released me in a slow descent down his body. It was torture and pleasure at the same time. "All night I've wanted to see how this dress looked on my floor."

I turned in his arms, exposing my back to him. "Let's answer that question."

He took his time guiding the zipper down. When he skimmed his hands against my bare back, my insides turned molten. He slid the garment off my arms and down my body. I rested a hand on his shoulder as he waited for me to step out of it. Even though removing the gown left me in a lacey corset and panties, I felt exposed like I never had with anyone else. Laurel's coveted gaze vanquished my vulnerability. Once I was clear, he tossed the dress to the front of the room and used his magic to guide it down to the floor. "Beautiful, but not as beautiful as you. And you were wrong."

I studied him as a grin formed on his handsome face.

"Red isn't my color. It's yours."

His message was a simple but important reassurance for me. I raised up on my tiptoes, kissed his cheek, and began working the buttons on his shirt. It would have been easier to undo them with magic, but I wanted to give him the same exquisite torture he had me. He kissed my temple as I slid his shirt off and took in his defined torso. The throbbing between my legs practically cheered me on to satisfy the craving to touch Laurel's skin. I ran my hands over his shoulders, down over his abs, and reached for his belt. His breath quickened with each movement I made. A scar marked the skin just above his navel. I assumed it was a battle scar and made a note to ask about it later.

He inhaled as I pushed his pants down his legs and held them for him. He stepped out of them, and I tossed them toward my dress and used my wind magic to guide them to twist with my dress. "Perfect."

"Perfect," he repeated, but he was looking at me. "You are the sweetness of a magnolia blossom after a spring rain. Strong and vibrant and beautiful. I have so much respect for how fearlessly you speak your mind. You are an incredible force, and I'm not sure you know that about yourself."

My heart fluttered in my chest with a rush of happiness. His words sounded like...love. It was too soon, of course, but no one had spoken to me like that before. None of my lovers. He saw me.

"I see you too," I said.

He guided me toward the bed, and we fell against it together. Laurel held his weight up by his elbows over me.

"I see you, Gemma." He placed his hand between my breasts and rested his palm over my heart, which was threatening to explode out of my chest. "I feel you."

"Then show me," I whispered.

His mouth devoured mine. He grazed my neck with his lips, cupping my breasts through the strapless fabric.

Warmth flooded me. My body ached with the need to be touched. I arched my back toward his chest, wanting the skin-to-skin contact.

He leaned back. A smirk crossed his face, and he flicked his wrist. The busk came undone. Laurel yanked it free and tossed it off the bed. My swollen breasts met his chest, and my nipples pebbled from the contact. He descended on my breast, licking and blowing, making my nipple so sensitive it was almost painful. I needed more friction, and I bucked my hips against him.

He nipped at my ribs as he moved lower down my belly. My breathing was so rapid I thought I would pass out as my need soaked my center. He snapped his fingers, and my panties were in his hand, swinging around one of his fingers. Laurel sniffed them and tossed them over his shoulder. "If I don't taste you, I'm going to explode. I bet you'll be sweet too."

My chest flushed. Heat radiated from me. *Goddesses and gods.*

He licked from one end of my sex up to my clit. I quivered while he savored my most sensitive spot. My eyes rolled back from the pleasure.

"I knew I was right." He hummed against me as he sucked down on my bundle of nerves.

Stars crowded in on my vision. I was close to unraveling. "I want you inside me."

"Oh, you're going to get more than one of these." He chuckled and slid two fingers inside, stroking the perfect spot. My toes curled. "Let yourself go, Gemma."

My vision blurred, and bliss erupted through my body. I shook with the intensity of the orgasm. I called his name, but my voice sounded so far away. The climax kept going, and I thrust my hips up. I'd never had one shatter me so completely. Laurel removed his fingers, and my eyes fluttered open. If I died and went to the next realm, I'd have experienced the most blissful moment thanks to him. Well, there was one more thing I wanted before I died.

I met Laurel's gaze, and an aftershock vibrated through me. He watched me intently. It was like we knew each other on a deeper level, and I felt happy in a way I hadn't in years. I pulled his face to me and caressed his lips with mine.

He ran the head of his cock over my sensitive nub. I jerked. He teased my entrance, and desire flooded through me again.

"I'm not done with you yet."

CHAPTER 16

CONNECTION
LAUREL

Gemma's slickness and her orgasm had almost made me come without a touch, and I was ready to bury my dick inside her. I shifted enough to wrestle out of my underwear. The fucker stuck on my ankle, and I had to flick my foot to get it free. All of Gemma's skin was soft, but the warm wetness when I put my fingers in her was the softest. I knew I'd never get enough of her then.

"I'm on the monthly contraceptive," I said, not sure if they even had it in the prison realm.

"I am too," she said, her voice a purr.

"And you have"—I swallowed hard—"you've done this before?"

Her eyes glittered like flames flickering to life. She laughed and stroked my cock in her hand. I throbbed against her palm. She ran her thumb through the precum and licked it. I gritted my teeth, almost coming undone at the sight.

"I have. You're not going to hurt me."

I positioned myself at her entrance. Her lids fluttered closed. "Open your eyes, Gemma. I want to see into your soul when I fuck you."

She met my gaze with a burning hot fire in her eyes. I connected to her and didn't need a bond like she had with Cyrus. We had our own tie, and I gave myself over to the link. My heart beat in time with hers.

I thrust into her wet, velvet-soft skin and paused to give her time to adjust. Holding back was not without difficulty. She wiggled underneath me, trying to take more. I gave it to her.

She moaned so loudly the sound vibrated my dick. I'd been on the edge the moment I'd entered her, and I bit down on my lip to hold back.

"Goddesses and gods, Gemma." I picked up my pace.

Gemma raked her nails down my chest, and the pain was the sweetest mix with pleasure.

I leaned forward and bit down on her nipple—not enough to draw blood but enough to intensify everything for her. She cried out in a way no one would interpret as anything but ecstasy, and her eyes rolled back. My strokes became erratic.

Gemma's breaths were panting moans, and each sound pushed me closer. I wanted to see her come with me. I reached my hand between us and rubbed my thumb in circles on her clit. Her pussy tightened around my cock, and I braced myself up with one arm. "Open your eyes, beautiful. You know what I want."

She opened her eyes as she screamed my name, and

the sheer pleasure in her voice sent me toppling over the edge of my orgasm. Her walls contracted around my cock in fierce spasms, like her personality did to my heart. I spilled my seed deep inside her, and it went on for what seemed like forever. I didn't want this to end. Satisfaction took over as the last drop filled her.

I looked down into her eyes, and she let me into the window of her feelings. Contented. Satiated. But there was something more. Something I'd suspected and wanted to explore—after she had time to recover.

I covered her mouth in a gentle dance as I maneuvered us into a position where I could hold her against me. Her breathing began to slow, and I stroked my fingers up and down her arm. "You are incredible in every way, Gemma."

She laughed and pinched my nipple.

"Ouch," I said, laughing with her. "What was that for?"

"That is possibly the most generic thing you could say to a woman after sex."

Had other men said that to her? Embarrassed I'd made her think anything less than how amazing being with her was, I shifted so I could look her in the eyes. "Really? I've never said it to anyone but you, and I've never felt that way before you."

She smiled and nibbled my shoulder. "That's better."

"How was it for you?"

"Incredible in every way." Her eyes widened as she mocked me.

"I'm two seconds away from kicking you out of the bed," I said, hiding my smile.

She grabbed my dick. I hardened immediately at her touch. While I recovered quickly, like most fae, that soon was unexpected. "Is that so? I was hoping for more of this incredible appendage of yours."

I laughed and shifted her on top of me. "Who am I to deny the request of the most beautiful woman I've ever seen?"

She paused and leaned forward, rubbing her breasts against my chest. "This beautiful woman wants you to know that was the best for her too."

I couldn't remember a time when I was so connected to a partner. The tie between us was taut like a string pulled tight. I pulled her against me and devoured her mouth.

CHAPTER 17

PANCAKES

GEMMA

Incredibly happy for the first time in so long, I snuggled against Laurel's chest and inhaled his earthy scent. If the world were perfect, we'd be able to stay in bed forever, but the world was far from ideal.

He kissed the top of my head. "Good morning. I'm glad you didn't sneak away during the night. I like waking up to you."

I considered going back to my room, and I thought about seeking Cyrus out to talk to him too. For some reason, I felt like I was betraying my bonded, even though that wasn't possible—at least not by sleeping with a fae. I didn't reach out to him through the shared link either and hoped none of the activities from last night seeped into our bond. It happened way too often between the time I was eighteen and twenty-one. After one particularly wild night, he told me. I'd been humiliated and infuriated with him, but he did teach me how to build a mental block. He probably hadn't intended me to be so good at it though.

"You okay?" Laurel's voice was gentle. "You're not regretting it, are you?"

He was concerned I thought it'd been a mistake, and that couldn't be further from the truth. I kissed his chest. "No, not at all. I'm happy to wake up next to you too."

"Why am I sensing a but?"

"No but," I said, and meant it. Being with him was different. I was different after last night. When he'd looked into my eyes, I'd known this wasn't some fling. A real connection, not all that different from my bond with Cyrus, existed between us.

He picked up his phone from the nightstand. "I'm going to order us some breakfast. Do you want anything special?"

"Do you have pancakes here?"

He smiled and typed away on the phone. "We do."

"That is one thing better here." I enjoyed how the mundane things were easier with the technology. When Ari and Drew were rescued and arrived, I'd have so much to show them.

"What's that?"

"Being able to order food to your room with that little thing."

"Is that the only thing that's better here?" He pushed me down on my back and hovered over me.

I bit back my smile. "Hmm...Yes, that's all I can think of."

"I was going to take a shower, but maybe I need to refresh your memory before breakfast arrives."

"Please go take your shower, and I'll go over to my

room to get dressed." I wanted a minute alone to check in with Cyrus and see if we were in agreement to stay. If he wanted to go back, I'd be torn.

Laurel glanced at my dress still tangled with his clothes on the floor. "Or you could grab something out of my closet."

The dress, a beautiful reminder of what led to this moment, was in no shape to be worn. Plus, morning had risen, and more casual attire would be better.

"Either way, I'll be here when you get out of the shower."

He kissed the tip of my nose and headed into the bathing chamber...bathroom, as they called them here. I heard the water start running and checked out what Laurel had that I might be able to wear. There was a button-up shirt that brushed the top of my thighs. Being in his shirt reminded me of last night and seemed right. I sat in the plush barrel chair by the window. The sun filtered in and warmed the space.

Cyrus?

Yes, do you need me?

I didn't know how to explain what I was feeling. Complete, but not. Happy but missing a part of me. Needing him here but knowing asking him to come would be wrong.

Just checking in. Where are you?

Rounding the corner of your hallway.

Shit. Guilt and panic killed my pancake craving.

Gemma? Are you okay?

Laurel had asked me the same thing, and I still wasn't

sure how to answer the question. *Yes, but I'm in Laurel's room, not mine. We're going to have pancakes. Join us?*

Amusement came down the bond. *I'm not sure I need to interrupt pancakes.*

I want you here, Cyrus.

Then I'm at the door.

The shower cut off. My timing sucked, but maybe we needed all of us present for the conversation. "Cyrus is here just so you know," I called through the door.

I looked down at the shirt I had on. Cyrus had seen me in a worse state of undress a time or two. The shirt would be fine. I crossed the suite and opened the door.

Cyrus stood in his human form, looking stern as ever. He looked me up and down. I had the urge to tug the hem of the shirt lower and smoothed my hair instead.

"Come in." I opened the door wide enough for him to walk inside.

He smirked. "Is this some new fashion statement in this kingdom?"

"No, but I appreciate your attempt at humor." I sighed.

His shoulders relaxed, but tension still bracketed his eyes. "What's on your mind? Are you second-guessing staying?"

"No, on the contrary. I don't think I could go home knowing it might mean my family would pay a price for my selfishness."

A knock at the door interrupted us. Laurel came out of the bedroom dressed. *Thank the goddesses and gods.* He nodded at Cyrus and gave my attire a glance and an approving wink. "I'll get the door."

Cyrus stared at me with a jovial expression, but I didn't see what he found so funny. The awkward silence built while Laurel chatted with the person at the door. He returned with a tray. "Who's hungry?"

"Me," I said, eyeing the cloches as he set them on the table.

Laurel grabbed some plates out of the cabinet.

I lifted one lid and found a mound of bacon. Cyrus was a vegetarian, so that would be a hard pass from him. I snatched a crispy piece for myself. Laurel lifted one of the lids to reveal the pancakes. They were just like I'd had at home, so some things were the same in his kingdom as mine. I forked a couple and put them on a plate.

Cyrus took a few for himself and Laurel did too.

"This is nice," I said, "eating breakfast with you two."

Laurel and Cyrus exchanged an unreadable look as if they expected the other to know what the hell I was talking about when I didn't even know.

"Tell us what is on your mind, Gemma," Cyrus said, putting his fork down with a clang.

"I..." I didn't have a clue how to start this conversation. Maybe this was a mistake. I hadn't asked Laurel about this first, and I hadn't talked to Cyrus to question if he even wanted to be with me. "Never mind. Let's just finish breakfast."

I chickened out, and they let me. Although it was a relief, I'd have to find the right time to have the conversation. We ate the rest of the meal in silence.

"Can we go back to your lab sometime?" I asked Laurel. "I want to look at some of the work there again."

Excitement twinkled in his eyes. "Of course."

"If you don't need me there, I have unicorn things to attend to."

I nodded, miffed the conversation would have to wait until another time. "I'd like to talk to you later when you are free."

"All you have to do is call for me." Cyrus scooted his chair back and patted my shoulder. The graze of a touch sparked the desire for more. "I'll see you later."

Laurel wore a contemplative expression on his face. He and I were alone again, and the only thing I'd accomplished was making things awkward.

I kissed him, gliding my lips over his in a promise. "I'm going to my room to take a shower and get dressed."

He nodded. "I need to make a few phone calls, so I'll be here whenever you are ready. My shirt looks good on you. Keep it."

I shut the door behind me and leaned against it, grasping the collar and inhaling Laurel's scent. Last night replayed in my mind, and I looked forward to repeating the end of our evening. A throat cleared at the other end of the hall, and I glanced over that direction to see who the noise belonged to, expecting to see Rain. Instead, I saw Merrick.

CHAPTER 18
THE MARK
GEMMA

What is Merrick doing coming out of Rain's room? Oh. Eww.* She sauntered down the hall toward me. I wanted to run to my room and shut the door before she got here, but that wasn't a mature way to handle the situation. So, I angled my body toward her with my hands on my hips in the biggest fuck-you stance I could muster. She wasn't going to get on my nerves today, especially not after I saw her leaving the room of the brother of the man she tried to claim as her fiancé.

Merrick looked me up and down like I was horse shit caked on her boot. I wished I had some to fling in her face. "You do not belong here."

My anger spiked, partly because I believed she was right but also because my mother told me and Ari to never let a bully make us feel like we were less than. "My mother gave her life for our people."

"These aren't your people. They don't know you."

"Neither do you."

"And I don't want or need to." Her eyes narrowed. "Laurel and I have been promised to each other since before you were born. You can't come in and fuck him into forgetting that commitment."

"So, you think fucking his brother is going to endear you to him?"

She invaded my space and stuck her finger in my face. "If you continue to put yourself between me and Laurel, I will take you down so far no one will care you are the daughter of a general given glory for a battle she didn't even fight in. Now that I think about it, you are a lot like her. She fucked the king for favor. Is Rain next on your list?"

My anger turned to rage the moment she defamed my mother. I might not have known the version of her that was General Daphina, but I knew exactly how strong she was. "Get your finger out of my face, Merrick."

"Or what?" She patted my cheek. "Nothing. Because you are nothing."

I summoned my wind and gave her a solid shove back. It didn't deter her. She walked right back into my space and grabbed my bare wrists. Pain erupted from her touch.

"Aagh." I tried to pull away, but her grip was firm. Blisters formed on my skin. Cyrus's training came back to me. I hooked my ankle behind hers and used the tiniest bit of wind magic to knock her off her feet.

Merrick tripped backward but stayed upright. She dove at me. "Urgh."

I moved away but not fast enough. She tackled me to

the ground. Her hands were around my throat, cutting off my air but not searing my skin like on my wrists. That might be next. I didn't panic. Cyrus trained me for this situation. I shoved my arms up between hers and wrapped my legs around her torso. She flipped easily, and I punched her in the jaw.

She connected a punch to my lip. "Get off me," Merrick screamed.

I landed another punch to her cheek. And another. "Do not ever touch me again and don't let me hear my mother's name or any reference to her leave your lips ever."

Hands were around my waist, pulling me away. I struggled.

"Sshh. It's me, Gemma." Laurel's soft tenderness wrapped me in calm.

Merrick jumped to her feet and lunged forward, but Rain grabbed her waist and hauled her back.

"I've got her. Take care of Gemma." Rain's gaze fell to my wrists, and the pain ratcheted up. I must have tuned it out when I fought Merrick.

"Fuck," I whispered.

"Fuck is right," Laurel said, scooping me up in his arms. "Let's go get you healed."

Merrick was screaming as Laurel carried me down the hall.

"I might have lost it on her," I said, choking back tears. I didn't want to cry here where someone might see me so humiliated.

"She has a way of bringing that out in people," he said, his tone full of venom.

"I shouldn't have hit her."

"Don't worry about Merrick. It's not the first time she's fought another woman, and I'm sure it won't be the last." He opened the door to a room. It wasn't his lab. There were screens, cabinets with vials and instruments visible, and carts with things on them I didn't recognize. He sat me on a weird bed with a thin mattress. The room had a sterile smell. "This is our med room. Technically, it's for Rain and me. It was originally built for the royal family, but Rain declared anyone could use it."

He was either nervous or distracting me or both. Either way, I found his demeanor endearing.

"I'm sorry I made a spectacle in your home." Father would have never let that happen at court. He would have considered it an embarrassment and sent me to court lessons or to muck the horse stalls like he did when I was a teenager. The customs here were different, so I didn't know how he'd want me to atone.

"You have nothing to apologize for. I know Merrick, and I don't even have to ask if she provoked it. I can see the evidence on your wrists and your lip." His voice was calm, but there were inflections of anger in his tone.

My wrists throbbed, and there wasn't a comfortable position for them. I swiped my thumb over my aching lip, and it came back with blood. Blood spotted my shirt. "Is this mine or hers?"

Laurel looked up from the tray he was prepping. "I think both. You got in a couple of good punches on her. That's not easy."

"You sound proud." My self-consciousness dwindled.

"Proud that my girlfriend defended herself against a bully?" He kissed my forehead. "Yes, I'm proud, but I don't like seeing you in pain. Wrists or lip first?"

I held up my wrists, and the pain came back in a nauseating wave. "Wrists."

"As you wish," he said. "This might hurt, but it heals fast."

He slipped my hand into his and pulled it toward him. I winced. The skin tightened on the burns from the healing my body had already started. He gently tapped an ointment on my skin from the tray where he'd mixed it.

"It's a mix of an aloe vera we curate and rosewater infused with my magic."

The relief was almost instantaneous, and the skin turned from an angry, blotchy red to a pinkish tone. "That's amazing."

His face relaxed. "And there shouldn't be any scarring since we got to it so fast."

"I'm not afraid of scars."

"I noticed the one on your knee." He gently set the hand he'd been working on down and picked up my other one, applying the ointment there.

"I fell off a horse when I first started learning to ride. Father insisted I carry the mark to remind me that even royals can face failure if we don't anticipate every possible outcome. Joke's on him since I'm not royal. I remember the day because it was so out of character for him. Guess that joke's on me." Looking back on what I'd learned, I'd seen a glimpse of the real person my father was.

Laurel set the other hand in my lap and wiped his

hands on a towel. "Don't let what you know now steal your memories of your childhood, whether those were good or bad, but especially the good ones." He cupped my cheek. "You didn't know who he was. He didn't even know who he was. You got the best version of him anyone will ever know, and that is yours to keep."

My eyes burned. I wanted to believe what he said because most of my memories with my father were good, and I wanted that to be what Ari and Drew got too. Laurel was far kinder than I'd given him credit for being when we first met. He was a good person—a really good one. "Thank you."

"Let's take care of that lip." He examined it. "It's just a small split and will probably heal in a few hours."

"I don't mind. It doesn't really hurt." I leaned into my training. Small scrapes would heal quickly on their own. No need to use our magic on them.

"Oh, I'm going to fix it too." He smiled. His thumb skimmed over the injury. Magic hummed from him and mingled with mine.

I'd never experienced a magical connection like this. It warmed until it melded like we were one. He ran his thumb over the spot again, and a tingle spread out from it. "Did you feel that?"

"I did. It was nice. Why can't all healing be like that?" It had never been...pleasurable for me. The previous times I required healing it was painful—how painful depended on how much healing was needed. A gift of Laurel's that the mending was gentle like him maybe?

"That wasn't how it usually goes." His eyes widened slightly.

I leaned back to get a good look at him and let the wall around my gift down. His aura was the same as when we met in the woods, but mine hung near it like a lost lover lingering for a touch. "Really? Why would it be different?"

"Your magic invited it. Like our power mixed."

"And that's never happened before?"

"No," he said, surprise in his voice.

"Maybe because we..." I trailed off short of saying the obvious. Sex changed things, but could it do that?

His brows pinched together. "I guess it could be possible. I've never had to heal someone I've had sex with."

"Never?" I laughed. It sounded so absurd we were discussing this.

He chuckled. "No. None of my partners have ever gotten in a fight in the hallway outside my apartments before either."

A twinge in my gut that I recognized as jealousy worked its way into my chest at the thought of him having other partners. I'd had my share, too, so it wasn't like I had a right to be jealous of his past. He'd said Merrick had been in fights, so...he hadn't been the one to heal her. Or maybe she hadn't been the one who needed healing from them.

"Ready to go get cleaned up and dressed for the day? I'd like to take you horseback riding if you are up for it."

"I'd love that. One of my favorite things is to ride."

He smirked.

"Horses." I blushed because there were other things I liked to ride and hoped the other was soon too.

CHAPTER 19
ALL DONE
LAUREL

Gemma was in her bath, and I'd found riding clothes that I laid out on the bed and then shut the door to her bedroom so she could have some privacy. At the door, a hard knock I knew was Rain's pounded through the wood.

I opened the door to my brother's concerned face. "Hey."

"Hey," Rain said, but he didn't come inside. "Merrick has some major bruises on her face. Gemma packs quite a punch."

"Merrick is lucky Gemma didn't use her magic. Why was she in your room, Rain?" I didn't care who he had in his bed, but she wasn't a good person. Her vindictiveness ran deep and was a wrath I didn't want to see anyone I cared about receive.

"Someone had to occupy her while you were fucking Gemma..."

I stepped into the hall and his space, closing the door behind me. "Careful, Brother."

"You are in love with her." Rain grinned like he did in our teens when we snuck out to the far side of the kingdom for one of the rougher bars. "I knew it."

I ignored his obvious elation. "Shut up, Rain. Why are you here?"

He gave me his classic are-you-stupid look. "Aren't you going to come heal Merrick?"

She'd attacked Gemma like the bully she was known to be. Nothing in me wanted to help her, which was unusual. My desire to help and heal outweighed my anger for others, but not with what occurred in the hallway. "No, I'm not."

"We can't send her home like this. Her father will be all up my ass. He might even think I did it, and that would be worse."

"I'm not doing it."

The door came ajar, and I reached back, connecting with something soft. Not the door. I glanced over my shoulder mortified to see my hand pressed against Gemma's stomach. "Sorry."

Gemma rested a hand on my arm. The shirt fell back away from her wrist, and the skin was still slightly pink but better with every minute. "Go heal her. That fight was as much my fault for letting her taunt me as it was hers for being a bitch."

She had more grace than her attacker. Merrick would have found a reason for the conflict whether it had been in the hallway or some other time.

Rain chuckled. "Don't let him run you off, Gemma. I like you."

She ignored him and studied me. Gemma looked beautiful, and I wanted to take her to bed and erase the memory. That would have to wait. "You have a gift. I'm not going to be jealous that you use it on her arrogant ass."

I wanted her by my side, not only to see there was nothing to be jealous of but because I wanted to be near her. "Come with me?"

She shook her head. "No, this is your deal. I might not be jealous, but I don't want to see her either. I need to talk to Cyrus anyway."

"I'm kind of surprised he didn't show up during the fight." He should have known she was hurt and come to her aid. Not that he was needed. She could undoubtedly handle herself. Gemma might have talked to him through her bond. My only experience with that was Rain and Casimir, and I wouldn't know unless he told me they were communicating.

"We can block each other out, and I..." Her cheeks blushed, and I had to shut down the throb in my pants.

"Did that last night?" Rain asked, smirking.

Gemma's neck flushed as bright as her cheeks, but she didn't look away.

"Why are you still here?" I shoved my brother's shoulder.

Rain backed away with his hands in the air. "See you in my room." He pointed in that direction and spun on his heels.

"It shouldn't take too long to heal her. I'll be back soon." I leaned forward and kissed her cheek.

"I'll be in my room waiting for that ride." Her cheeks deepened to a darker pink. It was hard to leave her looking so vulnerable. I reached out and twined my fingers with hers. As they slipped apart, I felt the absence.

My brother leaned against the frame of his door and pushed it open with his foot to make room for me to walk through. Merrick sat in a chair in the darkest corner of the living room. She looked beaten in spirit more than she did physically. There was a time I cared for her, but her actions over the years eroded those feelings. Her treatment of Gemma finished them off.

"Can you turn the overhead lights on so I can see her injuries, Rain?"

"You can speak to me," Merrick said, her tone like a snake's hiss.

"I can. Are you going to try to rile me up the same way you did Gemma?" I sat on the ottoman in front of her chair to assess her injuries. Merrick's bruises were nasty, even by fae standards—already turning a deep purple. The cut over her eye was starting to heal, and her nose looked like it might be broken and healing crooked. I'd start with it since it was the worst.

"She started it."

"Merrick, you and I both know that's not true. You've started more fights with other women than most men I know start with each other."

She huffed. "Do you know how embarrassing that was

to see her coming out of your room knowing we are to be married?"

That was rich considering she'd been fucking my brother.

"Rain, can you go get your med kit for me? I'm going to need it," I called out over my shoulder to my brother. His footsteps faded into the bedroom.

"We're not getting married, Merrick. You are going to have to accept that. There is nothing that will change it. Ever."

"I could have her sent away," she said, her voice thick. She was going to cry, but I wouldn't let her believe in a future that wasn't going to happen. My blood boiled she'd dared to threaten Gemma, but I let my empath powers feel her sorrow and hurt to stop myself from verbally obliterating her.

"No." I softened my voice. "You can't, and if you tried, I would have you exiled."

Tears streamed down her face. "What does she have that I don't?"

"My love," I said, admitting it for the first time and hating it was to her and not Gemma. But I knew that was the only thing that would end this.

She sniffed and wiped her tears away. Her attitude sucked, but she was tough. She would be fine and sink her nails into another noble for stature. I tasted the bitterness in her feelings, but acceptance sat right below it. This was the end.

Rain returned with the kit.

"This is going to hurt." I pushed gauze into her nose as I prepared to straighten it.

"Nothing could hurt more than what I'm feeling right now," she whispered.

I might have allowed myself to have guilt about her pain if she wasn't a master manipulator.

"I'll get some ice," Rain said.

A crunching sound broke the silence as I moved her nose into the right position and sent the healing energy to the needed place. It wasn't the same as Gemma—no magic mingling or connection. Merrick didn't flinch or make a sound. It was like she'd transported herself somewhere else, and I didn't blame her. I moved on to the cuts. They healed completely, confirming my thoughts the lacerations weren't too deep. The bruises were next, and I erased them with a gentle touch.

"All done," I said, making it final.

"Yes." She nodded. "All done."

I helped her to her feet, and she hugged me. It was different than the other times. It was a goodbye. Her closure was my relief.

"She's a good match for you. I hope you have a long life of happiness."

"And I wish you to find someone who can give you the life you want."

"Your car is waiting, Merrick," my brother said, handing her an icepack. "I'll walk you to it."

She took his extended arm, ignoring the offered ice, and didn't look back. A weight lifted from me like a threat had been defused, and all I wanted to do was get back to Gemma.

CHAPTER 20

THE POWER
GEMMA

Cyrus made it to my door in what seemed like seconds. He was in his human form. I was glad to see him, but I'd hoped it would take him longer to give me time to gather my thoughts. My fear I wouldn't follow through made me call him before I'd prepared myself.

He sniffed the air. "You've been hurt. I smell your angry blood and the healing magic on you."

My lip was healed, but there was still a faint trace of pink around my wrists. "I got into a little fight. You should see the other woman."

"I don't care about the other fae." He grasped my wrists in a light hold and examined them. His gentle caress excited me, and my chest heated with what was probably a bright flush. "Does it hurt?"

"No, Laurel used an ointment and magic to speed up the healing."

"It doesn't look as if it will scar." He lifted the inside of my wrist to his mouth and kissed it. His magic healing tingled along the marks and healed. His action was so unexpected I froze. Not only was it unheard of for a unicorn to heal a fae, even their bonded, but the touch was intimate. I'd thought about crossing the unwritten forbidden line of a bonded and their charge with him... until Laurel. If it had been before we came to this king-dom...I felt so confused. I wanted them both, but I'd just been with Laurel. He'd called me his girlfriend. Wasn't that a commitment that should stop me from wanting to fuck another? The thought of them both...at the same time...woke something sensual in my core. *No, it's a line that cannot be crossed, Gemma.* I shoved the idea back deep in my mind.

"Cyrus—"

He sniffed the side of my face and wrinkled his nose. "I smell him on you, and I don't mean his healing touch."

The unicorn's sense of smell left me mortified on more than one occasion but none more than him sniffing out the fact Laurel and I had sex. Not that he hadn't done it with other lovers I'd had but this was—

"Your scent is different."

His comment broke my trance, and I stepped back. The power in me had changed since Laurel healed me, or at least I noticed it then too—as if something new I couldn't quite touch yet was there from when our magic inter-twined. "How so?"

"You smell like you but something else."

"Like him?"

"Yes." An unreadable emotion flashed across his face and was gone before I could decipher it. "He approaches."

A knock came from the door. My moment alone with Cyrus would have to wait.

"Come in," I shouted.

Laurel entered and studied us. Dark circles covered the tender flesh under his eyes, and I wanted to kiss them away. He didn't cross the room, and I wondered what he saw that made him stall.

"All done?" I asked, forcing my voice to be normal.

"She'll live." He walked over and slid his hand around my waist.

Cyrus appraised our touch with interest that shifted to concern.

"You nearly killed someone, Gemma? I thought it was a scuffle."

I rolled my eyes. "It was minor. No one was near death."

Laurel squeezed my hip, and I leaned into the touch. "We're going to have to keep you two separated for a while because she blames you for me not marrying her."

"Would you have married her if I wasn't here?" I asked, glancing up at him.

"No, that was never going to happen," Laurel answered.

Cyrus shuffled. "Maybe I should go so you two can talk."

Now or never, Gemma Hemera. I almost giggled from nervous hysteria but composed myself before either Cyrus or Laurel seemed to notice. "No, don't go. I wanted to talk to each of you alone first, but since you're both here, there is something I want to discuss."

Laurel and Cyrus exchanged a guilty look, and I wondered what they had been up to that made them regretful.

"Did the cook..." Laurel's voice trailed off as he looked at Cyrus.

"Nothing happened," Cyrus shrugged. "We just ate sandwiches together."

"What are you talking about?" I asked, not understanding what food had to do with anything.

Laurel squinted his eyes and tilted his head slightly. "Are you not talking about us going to the kitchen together?"

"No, should I be?"

Laurel swallowed hard. "I..." He paused. "While we were eating sandwiches in the kitchen...I asked Cyrus if it was normal to have some level of attraction to the bonded unicorn of someone I was falling for."

"I see." I processed the information, secretly pleased some magnetism existed between them. If our powers were mixed, was this allure he had for Cyrus bleeding off of me? I looked at Cyrus. He lowered his eyes. I reached down our bond and felt his shame. He tried to shut me out, but I had my mental foot planted. "And what did you say as my bonded?"

He met my gaze with remorse in his eyes. "I told him that it'd been a long time since he'd been around a bonded unicorn and fae and that he might have forgotten what it was like."

"So, you lied?" I crossed my arms. My anger mixed with mirth, and I bit back a smile. All of us had the same interest in each other, and everyone had kept quiet. *What if I had lost my nerve today?*

Cyrus tilted his head to a weird position and shrugged. "Omitted a few details is more accurate."

Laurel pulled me to him, my back to his front. My body pressed against him soothed my nerves. He rested his chin on my shoulder. "Someone clue me in on what I'm missing?"

I looked up at him over my shoulder. "It is not a typical outcome for someone to be attracted to their girlfriend's bonded."

"Oh." Laurel's face twisted in confusion. "So, I'm genuinely attracted to your bonded. That's kind of awkward."

Enticing would be how I'd describe it. Laurel shifted behind me, and I was certain he had me in front of him to hide his growing dick. He seemed stimulated by the idea, too, and my courage and hope grew that my daydream might become reality.

"Her bonded is right here," Cyrus said, averting his eyes from us.

"Are you attracted to me too?" Laurel asked Cyrus, disbelief in his voice.

If Cyrus denied any attraction, then I'd let the discussion end here. But, if he confirmed the magnetism between the three of us, my fantasy could come true.

My bonded grumbled. "Gemma's allure for you comes down the bond, and it makes me interested."

"Maybe we need to get this out of our systems." I blurted my inner monologue out loud, ripping the bandage off.

They both stared at me and waited. Neither of them appeared disgusted by the idea or all that shocked, so I took that as my clue to continue.

I glanced at Laurel. "Before you and I were together last night, I'd had a couple of fantasies of being with you both at the same time. I think it might be my curiosity about my little fantasy causing this awkwardness between us."

Some fae relationships consisted of three members. When I snuck out, I saw some at the pub occasionally. I'd known my duty was to marry for the sake of the kingdom, so I'd never considered it for myself. The expectation died when I came to this side of the forest and learned I wasn't an actual princess. The freedom of my decision empowered me. I expected Cyrus and Laurel to stop the discussion anytime, but they both stayed and listened.

"Gemma, I've had this kind of experience before, and we need to set some ground rules so no one gets hurt," Laurel said, his thumb making small circles on my hip. "Maybe we should sit down and talk through those."

Jealousy curled around my stomach thinking of his past sexual experiences, but I'd had my own, too, and had to let that go.

"I agree," Cyrus said.

I gestured to the large couch. The relief that we were all three sitting down to talk through the fantasy loosened the tension in my neck. It didn't mean we were going through with it, but I wanted to believe we would. The thought of both of them together was bliss in my head, and I was curious if it would be in real life too. My biggest concern was it would ruin my relationship with both of them, and I couldn't live with that. I'd slept with Laurel, and our time together couldn't have been more perfect. There wasn't anything missing from that moment, but something in me thought Cyrus belonged with us. I couldn't ignore it either.

Laurel sat close to me and draped a casual arm behind me. Cyrus sat and faced us, just out of reach from me. The temptation to slip down our bond and see what he thought was difficult to ignore. He respected the boundary so I should too.

"First, we need to discuss what we want out of the experience. If we don't want the same thing, then we're going to have a problem down the road," Laurel said.

I shifted and glanced between them. If unicorns had threesome's I wasn't familiar with it, but I knew some participated with fae. It was pretty common among the fae to invite others from time to time. Some lived out their years together but never with a unicorn, so this had to be a one-time thing. That must be what Cyrus and Laurel were thinking too. I wanted to know just once what it was like to be with them. "Do we all agree that it's to get this three-way attraction out of our systems?"

"Works for me," Laurel said, curiosity in his eyes.

"Yes." Cyrus's tone was a little broody, which I knew without even reaching down the bond meant he was uncomfortable. Unease passed down the bond like a tidal wave, but it was from fear. He was worried about me. I sent reassurance back to him that this was what I wanted. The tension didn't disappear, but his face relaxed.

"I know that Laurel and I are both on pregnancy prevention medicine, but I don't know about unicorn and fae. Do we need to do anything else?"

Cyrus's cheeks brightened. He shimmered like he wanted to shift to his natural state but solidified back to his fae form. It was the first time I'd seen him embarrassed. "No. A unicorn can't get a fae woman pregnant, to my knowledge, and we don't share any diseases, so there shouldn't be concern there."

"That's good," I said. There were certain things I'd tried in a past experience I had no intention of repeating. Ever. Hopefully, it wouldn't be a deal breaker for either of them. "What about acts we don't want to do?"

"I don't have any limits," Laurel said. "I'm good with it all. What is on your boundary list?"

"Nothing goes in my ass—fae, unicorn, or otherwise. That's my only request." I'd bled for two days after my experience several years ago and not even the two gorgeous male specimens in front of me could tempt me.

"Noted," he said. "I meant what I said. I'll try anything at least once."

I shouldn't have been surprised Laurel was such a free spirit, but I was. No one, fae or unicorn, would describe Cyrus the same, and I knew little of his sexual experience outside of the pairing he had with Leana. While I never shared it with anyone, I'd picked up on how they were appearances-only in their relationship—

an assigned pairing by his brother. "What about you, Cyrus?"

"I don't want to be in my unicorn form, but if we all agree and the moment is right, I'll offer my horn to increase the pleasure." Cyrus's tone showed interest.

Unicorns were protective of their horns because they could provide pleasure or death by piercing the skin. I hadn't expected him to offer something so intimate, but it did let me know he wanted this as much as I did. "What if things get to be too much?"

"We use a signal for us all to stop," Laurel said. "A word. You choose it, Gemma."

"How about 'sprite?' They were nasty little bastards from what I've heard, so if something gets uncomfortable or out of bounds, I can't think of a better word."

Cyrus chuckled.

"Works for me," Laurel said.

"Same," Cyrus said. "I think you should lead, Gemma."

"Me?" I'd never had sex with two people at once and definitely not a unicorn and another fae at the same time. It frightened me, but there was more excitement than fear.

"He's right," Laurel said. "This is your fantasy. You lead."

"I thought we'd all been feeling this attraction?"

Laurel and Cyrus exchanged a look, and Laurel shrugged. He took my hand in his and kissed my fingertips. "You should have the power in this situation."

"Okay," I said and hoped I could live up to the role, but the pressure overwhelmed me. I needed a break from the tension to reset. "It feels kind of forced and awkward to just jump in now. What if we meet back here tonight?"

"I like that because we can still go see the horses as planned."

I smiled at Laurel, thankful we'd have some time alone before we did this. The warmth building in my chest seemed equal for both, and I needed to understand that. "Cyrus, are you good with that?"

"Yes, tonight is fine," he said with no animosity in his voice.

"I'd invite you to join us, but we're going to ride horses. I know that is not your thing." I leaned forward where I could reach his knee and patted.

He looked where I touched him and back at me with a smile. "I figured from your attire." He stood. "I'll walk with you to the stables. I need to go talk to a friend in that direction."

CHAPTER 21

WHISPERER

GEMMA

C yrus was quiet on the walk to the stable, but he stayed close to me, excusing himself after a brief goodbye. I watched him walk away along the edge of the palace grounds, releasing his glamour and returning to his natural form with the white coat shimmering in the sunlight. His black mane and tail blew in the breeze and his scent of woods and power wafted around me, a reminder of the strength of the gold horn parting the hair of his forehead. A rush of desire pooled in my belly remembering what he offered to do with the horn. My fantasy hadn't changed since our talk. If anything, the discussion reinforced my hunger for them both. Laurel slipped his hand into mine and kissed my temple, and I relished the sweetness of the gesture.

"You're still my girlfriend, right?" he whispered in my ear. It was intimate but unnecessary considering Cyrus was now out of sight.

I looked at him, confused by the question. "Yes, why wouldn't I be?"

He brushed a strand of hair off my face. "Checking to make sure the conversation with the three of us hadn't changed how you feel."

"No, Laurel. Not at all. It's just like...a one-time thing we need to do and get past. Then all the awkwardness can go away and we can be normal together." I squeezed his hand. If anything, I worried more if his feelings might change. What if he and Cyrus connected in a way that I was out? My heart would be broken.

"Good." His face wore a neutral mask, but I could see the worry under the surface.

"I'm excited to see the horses."

The horses were a welcome distraction, and I wondered if I would be able to communicate with them like I could in my kingdom...former kingdom...prison. I didn't know what to call it. Mother had said equine communication was a gift her mother had. Mother supposedly didn't get it because it tended to skip a generation.

"They should be saddled and ready to go." He led me through the stable. Hay and straw scented the air along with the other barn aromas. A couple dozen stalls lined each of the two halls. A few horses slept. I didn't want to open the conversation with so many at one time, but I listened for them. None spoke to me. While it didn't surprise me, disappointment made me doubt my ability.

"Are these all yours and Rain's?"

"Mostly. Some belong to other residents like our

cousins." We emerged at the end of the barn. There were two fine brown horses saddled for us in a pen with the gate open. In the paddock next to it stood a wild gray mare and a tall fae woman trying to tame the stunning horse.

"She's beautiful," I said. "But that fae is going to either hurt the mare or get hurt herself."

"The fae is Tealana. She's our trainer and usually has no issues in training the horses. Persephone is a special case."

"Special how?"

"I rescued her from the vampire lands. They had been feeding on her. She doesn't like to be touched. Tealana has been working with her for months."

Shock contorted my features before I could stop it. Months without improvement meant Tealana was missing something.

"That's heartbreaking." We walked toward the exercise area.

Tealana noticed us and opened the gate to exit. Persephone barreled toward the opening. Tealana struggled to get the barrier closed, but Persephone leaped in the air and cleared them both. The horse barreled straight for us.

I opened my power and surrounded her with a bubble of wind, shutting out all the external noise. She and I were secured in there. Coaxing my wind into a comforting touch, I urged it to settle the mare's nerves. "You are safe here, Persephone."

"No. They will consume me." Her tone was frantic, the words running together so fast I had to concentrate to understand. Her panic-stricken vibrations overwhelmed me, and I focused on steadying my breath.

I summoned the soothing voice my mother had taught me to use with frightened animals. I'd even used it on my sister a time or two. "There are no vampires here. You are with the fae and safe. You have my word. Could a vampire understand you and you them?"

A shiver ran through her body, and she relaxed. "You have the gift."

Pleased with myself, I smiled. "I do."

She took slow steps toward me, and I held my hand out. She nuzzled it. "You are fae."

"I am, and so are the others. You are safe." I ran my hand over her cheek and down her neck. "You have recovered physically from your abuse?"

"Yes," she said. "I feel as if I know you. Your gift is so rare."

"I know. I've never met another like me who can speak to your kind." I ran my hand over her back and reversed toward her head. "Better?"

"Yes," she said. "I choose you to be my rider."

I laughed. Horses could be temperamental to fae, but I sensed a connection. It wasn't like the bond Cyrus and I had between unicorn and fae, but it existed in its own way. "Are you ready for that?"

"No one else but you, fae." She laid her head over my shoulder in a hugging motion.

"My name is Gemma."

"Only you, Gemma."

As honored as I was by her declaration, it was problematic given I didn't know what my role would be in the kingdom and if I would have time for her. "I'm going to release the wall I put around us, and when I do, all the sounds from the outside will come rushing back in. Are you ready for it?"

"As long as my new friend is with me."

"I'm here." I pressed one hand against her neck and released the protective wall with the other.

Persephone remained calm. Laurel and Tealana stared at me. Tealana's mouth gaped open, but Laurel looked impressed. A bit of pride swelled in my chest.

"You are an animal whisperer," Laurel said.

"I am." I nodded, feeling more like myself since I'd crossed the forest. "My new friend here is ready for a run."

"She's not broke yet," Tealana said.

"She doesn't need to be broken. Riding a horse is about trust. They need to trust that the rider isn't going to hurt them. Persephone and I have that trust."

"Let me take her, Princess Gemma. You should ride the trail horse we have saddled. Persephone could hurt you." She reached for the lead on Persephone's halter. Persephone backed out of reach and moved behind me.

"I don't want to go with her, and I don't want you to ride that hateful trail horse."

"Hateful, huh?" The trail horse knickered and kicked the fence of the paddock.

"Very rude." Persephone bobbed her head up and down.

"Point me to Persephone's saddle. She's made her decision, and it doesn't involve causing me injuries." I reached up to pat her neck, and she hung her head over my shoulder.

Tealana shook her head, her long braids swinging from the movement, and headed into the stable. "I'll get it for you."

"Do you want to meet my boyfriend?" I asked Persephone.

"Only if he's nice."

"He is." I took a step toward Laurel, and Persephone took every step with me. "Laurel, Persephone has agreed to a real introduction."

He held his hand out.

"Persephone, this is my boyfriend, Laurel."

"I smell him on you," she said, extending her nose to his hand.

"Does he meet your approval?" I asked her.

"Yes," she said. "Can we go run now?"

Tealana emerged with the saddle and other tack.

"As soon as you have a saddle on so I can sit."

"You put it on. I don't want her to touch me." Persephone had trust issues, but I didn't think Tealana had been cruel to the mare. She had a lot of horses to care for though, and Persephone needed someone to focus on her.

"Can Laurel help?"

"Yes." She shook her head up and down.

"She approves of you," I said to Laurel. "And you get to help me saddle her."

"Do I want to know what else she said?" Laurel asked, taking the saddle and blanket from Tealana.

"She thinks you're okay," I said, laughing.

SUSAN PERSON

I took the reins from Tealana who looked resigned but skeptical about whatever fate was ahead of me with the horse. "Thank you."

"Do you need anything else?"

"No, but you can unsaddle the trail horse. I won't be riding her today."

Tealana nodded and headed for the mare while we finished getting the tack on Persephone.

"Want me to give you a leg up?" Laurel asked.

"No." I slipped my foot into the stirrup and took a little hop, swinging my right leg over Persephone's back. I winked at Laurel. "I've got this."

A big smile broke across his face. "I see."

Persephone followed him over to his horse without any coaxing. I patted her neck and tried to communicate with Laurel's horse, but there was no response. "How's the saddle? Are you comfortable?"

"I'm not stressed if that's what you are asking."

"Good," I said, glad I wasn't causing her any anxiety.

Laurel mounted his horse. "I thought we'd take the trail to the west."

"Lead the way," I said to him, and then to Persephone said, "If you get scared or nervous, tell me."

"I'll be fine as long as you are here, Gemma." Trees created a canopy of varying shades of green over the path ahead.

Laurel clicked his tongue, and his horse broke into a trot down the well-worn trail. Persephone followed suit with no fear.

CHAPTER 22
HUNGER
LAUREL

Gemma was a godsdam horse whisperer, and not only that but she was also riding the horse no one could get close to. I wondered if she could talk to other animals. Some with the gift could, but others had an animal they were closest to. Horses appeared to be her affinity, and that was as rare as her beauty.

"What are you thinking?" she asked as we meandered our way back toward the stable.

"How impressive you are, Gemma."

She laughed. "Why would you say that?"

"Because it's true." I leaned over, and she met me half-way. Our lips tangled in a dance that held a promise—one I planned to collect on later.

I repositioned myself in my saddle. My horse nickered. Persephone nipped at him.

"What's up between them?"

"Well, my new friend?" she asked Persephone.

The gray mare neighed a few times.

Gemma blushed, and I wasn't sure if it was for her or Persephone. "I take it you were not interested."

Persephone made a few softer nickers.

"What did she say?" I asked Gemma.

Amusement lit up her face. "Apparently, he wanted to hook up with her later, and she declined."

"Awkward." I kicked his sides to move him into a trot. "I think this ride is over."

"Want to race them?" Gemma said to Persephone. She responded by taking off in a full run.

My horse and I were on their heels in a dead heat heading into the pasture. The pen came into view. A unicorn form took shape beside it, and it had to be Cyrus. He looked good in either embodiment. I preferred him in his human persona, but he was incredibly handsome either way.

Inside the pen, I dismounted my horse and hurried to help Gemma off Persephone just to be able to touch the woman in the saddle.

"I thought I'd wait for you to return," Cyrus said. "How was the ride?"

He was being nice. I wasn't sure how to respond. "Interesting."

"Meet Persephone." Gemma smiled at Cyrus. She shone like the bright sun overhead.

Cyrus glamoured into his faelike form. "Hello, Persephone."

The horse greeted him with a head nudge to his hand.

I slowed, shortening my stride, unsure what to say next. All thoughts had left my brain. Seeing Gemma and Cyrus both so close together conjured images I wanted but couldn't acknowledge. *Divert, Laurel. Offer food. The default.*

"Who's hungry?" I asked, my stomach growling to punctuate my hunger.

"Sandwiches?" Cyrus smirked.

His playfulness was new. Anticipation coiled around my cock. Gemma glanced between us. Her lips parted slightly. She uttered her quick goodbyes to Persephone and promised to visit tomorrow. When Gemma turned to see me and Cyrus waiting patiently like her lap dogs, her mouth quirked up.

"Shall we go have a sandwich then?" She hooked an arm through each of ours.

I pulled my phone out and texted some requests to the kitchen. "Your room or mine, Gemma? Or we could go to the kitchen if you prefer."

She thought for a moment. A mischievous grin broke across her face. "Mine."

"We'll have a meal and snacks for..." I swallowed. My hunger morphed into desire. "Whenever we need them."

The air electrified around us as if it anticipated what was to come.

"I want to take a bath first," Gemma said. "I smell like Persephone and sweat."

"Not a bad smell." Cyrus chuckled. The sound, a deep baritone, made heat rise in my chest.

"I don't think I've ever seen you so jocular." Gemma

gave Cyrus some side-eye. "You're usually so grumpy everyone gives you a wide berth."

Cyrus shook his head. A big smile spread across his face—warm and inviting. The images from before returned to my mind, and I wanted to please both him and Gemma.

"A shower wouldn't hurt me either," I said. The guards held the door open for us.

"Since you two will be occupied with your cleanliness, I'm going to run an errand I've put off. I'll meet you in Gemma's room," Cyrus said, backing away from us.

"Going to bathe in a stream?" I asked, picturing water running over his tall form and down over his broad chest.

Cyrus turned his back on us, and his hand went up in a gesture I'd often given my brother.

"Is he..."

Gemma looked over her shoulder at Cyrus. She stifled a laugh. "That's just his unicorn fist."

"His what?"

"You know I hate that term, Gemma," Cyrus grumbled.

"Precisely why I keep saying it." She let her laugh go.

The joyous sound trickled over me until it wound in my chest and around my heart. She'd found a way to capture a piece of me, and I knew I'd struggle to let her go when the time came. She'd said she would stay. Even though I believed she meant it, I, also knew firsthand what family allegiance could do. I walked her to her door.

She leaned back against it. "You could come shower with me."

The temptation was almost more than I could bear. I could take her against the door. "There is no way I would be able to wait for Cyrus if I did," I said. "And you're going to need your strength."

"You're the one who was hungry."

"Oh, I'm still hungry. My appetite is going to be hard to satisfy."

"That's a challenge I'll accept." She looped her arms around my neck.

I fought the urge to push my hips against her and show her there was no challenge. My cock strained against my pants. Instead, I lowered my head and brushed my lips against hers. She opened her mouth, and I deepened the kiss. Giving in to my lust a little, I backed her up to the door and pressed my hardness against her center. If I didn't break the kiss, Cyrus was going to find me making love to her on the floor of the hall. The thought of him watching, or even better, joining us made my arousal painfully potent. As much as I wanted to give in to a hall fantasy, I wanted to save all my desire to feast on both Gemma and Cyrus with all my strength.

I begrudgingly broke the embrace and kissed her nose. "I'll be back before you know it."

She grasped the handle as if she needed support. "I doubt that."

I watched as she closed the door. *Damn.* She was everything I'd dreamed of and more. I hoped that this fantasy indulgence didn't change anything for us. There had been an attraction between Cyrus and Gemma before I saw her in the woods. I was sure of it. If they hadn't come here, would they have ever explored it? The last thing I wanted was to be the third wheel. Gemma wasn't the type to not fight for what she wanted, so our future was in her hands. I was already hers if she wanted me.

CHAPTER 23

CONTROL

I stared at myself in the mirror, contemplating my choice. *Am I really doing this?* I opened the jar on the counter and sniffed. A familiar sweet, floral scent mixed with vanilla filled my nose. I applied the moon-flower cream to my entire body, and the mixture soaked in quickly. My skin shimmered as if it craved the touch of the two males waiting in the other room. I tamed my hair, smoothing it with just a slight curl at the end. Focusing on the details calmed my nerves. The fantasy was mine, but it was theirs too. Once we lived out this moment, everything would go back to normal. Cyrus would be my friend and my bonded, and Laurel would be important to me. Every-thing was still so new with him, and I didn't want him to think he wasn't significant just because I'd known him for a shorter time. Despite my repetitive reminders to myself, I wasn't sure I believed it would go back to what had been the status quo...or that I even wanted it to.

Wrapping the silk robe around me, I tied the belt and

listened to their hushed voices. They'd been there for some time together, and though I couldn't make out what they said, I could tell by the tone the conversation was lighthearted. I blew out a long breath. The casual exchange between them relaxed my nerves and reinforced my courage.

Cyrus and Laurel stood around the table full of food. Laurel held a freshly bitten apple in his hand. He dropped it on the table as he looked me over and licked his lips. His unbuttoned shirt exposed his perfect chest and abs. I drank him in and want pooled low in my belly. Cyrus had a strawberry in his hand and took a bite. He wore a light, summer-weight tunic and standard training pants that accentuated his muscles. I watched him lick the juice from his lips, his eyes never leaving mine, and my desire ratcheted up higher.

"Remember you are in control, Gemma," Cyrus said, slow-stepping around the table. "But I am asking you what you want. I've been able to read your thoughts for so long and yet I have no clue what you want here."

"I want both of you." I loosened the belt and shimmied the silky fabric off my shoulders until it slid to the floor, pooling around my feet.

The vulnerability twisting in my gut was chased away by the heated look Laurel and Cyrus shared. Laurel moved first. He dropped his shirt and stalked toward me like he was the predator and I the prey. He slid his hand over my collarbone and around my neck until his fingers slipped into my hair. His tongue licked up the lobe of my ear. Warmth simmered in my center.

"Gemma." My name sounded like a prayer on his lips. "Are you sure?"

"I've never been more certain."

Laurel gently turned me, so my back was to his front. He pressed a hot kiss to my shoulder and kneaded my breasts.

I crooked a finger at Cyrus. He watched with a molten stare, tugging his tunic over his head. Taking in his defined abs in a different way than when we trained, my legs went weak. I turned my face toward Laurel. He ran a thumb over my cheek, and I pressed a kiss into his palm. *This is really happening.*

Cyrus knelt at my feet. Unicorns kneeled for no one, but he gazed up at me from on his knees. I ran a hand through his hair. His eyes drifted closed as his hand caressed my calf. Laurel tipped my chin in his direction and devoured my mouth. Unfiltered desire radiated down my bond with Cyrus. He trailed his hand up the back of my leg and gripped my rear. Laurel tucked my hair behind my ear and trailed his lips from my temple to my jawline, sliding his hands down my side to grasp my hips. Cyrus nudged my legs apart, licking from my opening to my apex. My entire body shook. The intensity was so overwhelming and not enough at the same time. I gripped Cyrus's hair in one hand and dug my nails into Laurel's backside with the other. Laurel slipped a hand to my breast. His thumb brushed across my nipple, and I moaned into his mouth. He and Cyrus echoed the sound at the same time. I needed them both inside me—to have them both as close as possible.

Cyrus stood, guiding me to face Laurel. Each pressed their hardness against me, and their pants were a barrier I wanted gone. I reached for Laurel's waistband and undid the button, thrusting my hand inside to feel the velvet-like skin. He swore and worked his pants the rest of the way down, kicking them to the side. I shifted so I could take in both of the men. My heart thudded hard against my chest. Cyrus had his pants half down. Not letting go of my hold of Laurel's dick, I took Cyrus's impressive member in my other hand. A hiss escaped from his mouth. I moved my hands in unison, mesmerized by the way both Laurel and Cyrus writhed under my touch. My thighs dampened. I pulled my lovers closer. The air was so thick with desire I no longer knew where mine ended and theirs began.

Cyrus freed himself from my hand. I whimpered at the loss, but he positioned me, pulling my back to his front. His hardness pressed against my lower back. Laurel stood in front of me, locking our gazes with a lecherous stare. He looked feral, but there was more there. I quivered under the weight of the emotion. He ran the head of his cock through my slickness and over my sensitive clit. Sparks of pleasure shot through me. Cyrus's hand gripped my hip. His other rested on my neck as his thumb traced circles. Laurel ran his free hand up my arm until his hand found Cyrus's. He paused, then gripped Cyrus's wrist. Laurel met my gaze with an unspoken promise, and I thought we'd both explode from the ferocity.

He lifted one of my legs. Sliding inside in a slow smooth stroke, Laurel waited for me to adjust. I bit down on my lip from the pleasure and dropped my head back against Cyrus's chest. He nipped at my shoulder, drawing a gasp from me. My thoughts were filled with hedonistic desires like I'd never experienced before and some other emotion I couldn't quite name. Laurel leaned forward, and he and Cyrus locked in a kiss. Their lips parted, tongues winding together. Heat filled my body, my chest flushing with the need for release but not wanting the moment to end either. I reached behind me and stroked Cyrus's dick. Laurel lifted my other leg and wrapped it around his hip, until I was suspended between him and Cyrus. It somehow made the connection deeper. Cyrus skimmed his hand over my ass until he found where Laurel and I were connected. Laurel pinched my nipple, eliciting sparks of pleasure. I cried out. My pussy tightened around him. His mouth was on mine swallowing my cry.

Laurel found Cyrus's lips again. I slid a hand around each of their necks, partially for balance but mostly... *Goddesses and gods, I can't get them close enough.* My bonded slipped two fingers in, stretching me—prepping me. An ache formed in my core, because as good as his fingers felt, I had to have more. A primal need for them both to claim me together consumed me. Laurel's cock jerked. The sensations were everywhere, and my pussy throbbed for more. The men broke their kiss. Laurel found my mouth first, capturing it like I wanted them to claim my body. When he pulled away, Cyrus's mouth replaced the contact. Our bond erupted with passion and wantonness, and I was certain Laurel's joined ours. Maybe Cyrus's magic could allow him in for this moment. Fingers stroked my breasts, my nipples, and inside me—their touches gentle but demanding. I wanted to be ravaged until there was nothing left.

"More," I said, my voice raspy and not like my own.

"You feel incredible. Soft and wet, and I can't wait to see the look on your face when Cyrus enters you." Laurel's voice was a deep and soft caress like the discarded silk had felt on my skin. Any nervousness I still had disappeared. Laurel's arms were safe, and Cyrus would never hurt me... unless they planned to let me die of carnal cravings in their arms. My bonded removed his fingers. Laurel hooked his arms under my knees, cradling my ass in his hands.

Cyrus positioned his dick, brushing the head against where Laurel and I were joined. "Are you ready?"

"Yes," I pleaded. This was the moment I'd dreamt of, and the perfection of it prompted me for the final piece. If we only got this one time... "The horn too. I want it all."

He pushed just the tip of his cock in. The stretching was harsh, but not painful, and my head fell back. He lifted my hand, angling it to allow the tip of his horn to penetrate the flesh of my palm. A thrilling inferno radiated out from me. Laurel's mouth was on my breast, and he raked his teeth over the turgid peak. His name drifted across my lips. Cyrus pushed further in, holding my hips to keep me steady. I squirmed from the fullness but also from the intense craving to find completion.

"Good girl." Laurel's praise came in a hot breath on my skin. He licked between my breasts. "You're so beautiful." He trailed his mouth up until he found my lips. Our tongues entwined.

"So beautiful," Cyrus echoed. He and Laurel began to

move in unison, and the sensual dance rocketed my desire. So much. So good. I dug my nails into Laurel's shoulder with one hand and Cyrus's hip with the other.

Cyrus grunted something inaudible, and I thought it was one word...*mine*. He probably meant his charge or for the moment, but whether I'd imagined it or not, I let the word seep into my desire. I wanted both Cyrus and Laurel to claim me in every way.

"Are you okay?" Laurel asked, his teeth gritted together as if his restraint reached the breaking point.

"Don't stop," I said, light splintering in my vision. My body vibrated on the edge of climax. "I'm going to come."

"I'm close." Cyrus slipped a hand up my side, his fingers caressing the underside of my breast. His thumb grazed my nipple.

"Same," Laurel echoed.

Their thrusts quickened and went deeper.

The three of us met our pinnacle together, and a strangled mix of swears and promises filled the air in a symphony of pleasure. My orgasm erupted in color like auras or the sky—pinks, blues, oranges. Laurel and Cyrus both thrust the deepest they had been, hitting a spot of ecstasy. Shoot stars took over my vision. Warmth spilled into me. The connection stoked the fierce heat in my heart for both of them. They both belonged there. Cyrus kissed my shoulder. I collapsed against Laurel. We stood like that, me sandwiched between them, for what seemed like a long time. Cyrus pulled out first, leaving me half empty. Laurel went next, gently lowering my legs. I missed the closeness as soon as he did. I immediately wanted them both back inside me. Their seed spilled down my thighs. My legs threatened to give out on me, and Laurel scooped me up, carrying me to the bedroom.

He set me on the soft comforter and kissed my cheek. "Be right back."

I lay on my side, tired and so satiated. Cyrus lay behind me. He ran his hand from my thigh up my side. We'd said this was to get it out of our systems, but as satisfied as I was, I imagined having moments like this again.

Cyrus brushed the back of his fingers against my cheek. "You are exquisite. Thank you."

I sighed. "That was...unprecedented."

He chuckled against my shoulder. "Indeed."

Laurel returned with a warm, damp cloth. "Let me clean you up."

Cyrus kissed my temple. "I'll run a bath for you."

"I don't know if I can move." I ran a finger along Laurel's strong jawline.

Concern etched his face. "Did we hurt you?"

"No, I'm so satisfied I don't want to budge."

His face relaxed, and a smile turned up the corners of his mouth and eyes. He cleaned between my legs. Once he was done, he lifted me. "We wouldn't want to disrupt your moment."

I laughed as he carried me to the bathroom. Steam coated the mirror, and I disliked that our reflections were obscured. I wanted to see the three of us together.

Cyrus ran his fingers through the water. He gave me a soft smile. "It's perfect for you."

That word was the right one. Everything was perfect.

Laurel held me over the tub and lowered me. "Do you want to test it first?"

I dipped a toe in. The water was exactly right, but I ran my fingers through to double-check. "You can set me on my feet. I'll lower myself in."

Cyrus dropped some lavender into the water. "Relax. We're going to prepare some of the food for you."

"If I'd known having a threesome would get me treatment like this, I would have suggested it sooner." I lowered myself into the tub. Another conversation needed to be had because I had no intention of letting either of them go.

Laurel laughed. Cyrus kissed my forehead and nodded at Laurel. Laurel leaned forward, skimming his fingers over the water and letting it drip on my breasts. "You are magnificent, Gemma, in every way. I plan on reminding you of that often." He dipped his chin to kiss me, a soft, gentle dance of our lips.

I watched them walk out the door, closing it as they left. I hadn't thought the kind of happiness in my heart would ever be mine.

CHAPTER 24
RAY OF SUN
LAUREL

B y the time I walked into the front room, Cyrus had
dressed. I guessed he'd used unicorn magic to do
it so fast. He put plates on the table for the three
of us and went back to the stove to stir the pot he'd put on
the burner. I picked up my clothes and took my time situ-
ating them. I'd enjoyed being with him and Gemma
together, but as mind-blowing as it was, I relished my
time with Gemma alone too. Both felt right, but there was
a connection with Gemma that was more. No regrets
lingered, at least for me, but Cyrus seemed a bit off. I
joined him in preparing the food.

He and I set the table with the meal the kitchen had
sent up earlier in the day, and I sensed a wall that wasn't
there earlier. If I made myself vulnerable to him, perhaps I
could break through. I seized the opportunity to see where
his head was. "I love her, Cyrus."

"I know. I knew the moment I noticed her magic had

mingled with yours." He focused on his task of heating the potatoes.

"Have you heard of that happening before?" I'd expected him to say he loved her too. Maybe I had misread what happened between us during our moments of passion.

"Occasionally, when the love is strong." He looked up at me. Hurt filled his gaze—no animosity or anger.

I wanted to kiss him and reassure him, but I hadn't been around a bonded dynamic in over two hundred years. I didn't know what was appropriate.

His dark eyes glimmered. "And yours is."

My heart sped up. It was love. Real love. I wanted to ask if it extended to him, but that crossed a line he didn't appear to be ready to step over. "Thank you for telling me."

"I only told you what your heart already knew. As for hers, she will need to tell you." Cyrus's tone was resigned and sad as he headed for the door.

"Where are you going? She'll be crushed you are gone."

"I have unicorn business." He opened the door. "And she has you."

I leaned against it to prop it open. "What do you want me to tell her?"

"That you love her." He smiled, distant and unreadable, and patted my shoulder.

I watched him walk down the hall. My disappointment at his departure caught me off guard. Unicorns weren't exactly known for cuddling, and I wasn't looking to snuggle him. Still, his leaving hit me in the chest. I thought about what he said, still concerned about how Gemma would take his leaving. Was I ready to tell Gemma I loved her? I hadn't known her that long, but I understood the emotion in the same way the sun rose and set. It was like I'd known her my entire two hundred and twenty-five years.

The evening light cast its glow across the apartment like it were my answer. Then, as if Nyx herself appeared, Gemma emerged from the bedroom. The dusty rose silk robe from earlier wrapped around her, and the pinkish-orange rays of the setting sun bathed her in light. She was my everything.

I kicked the door shut and went to her, encasing her in my arms. She wrapped hers around me, nestling her head into the crook.

"Where's Cyrus?" She lifted her head. A concerned expression crossed her face.

"Unicorn secrets. He said he'd come back later. Are you disappointed?"

She lifted her shoulders in a small shrug, but I didn't miss the dejection in her gaze. "Kind of, but this is normal Cyrus behavior. He's pretty secretive."

"But you've never had sex with him before." I kissed the top of her head. She tightened her hold on me. She might not be ready to say it, but his leaving bothered her. "Hungry or bed?"

She tilted her chin up, her gaze meeting mine. "Bed."

I reached for her waist and lifted. She wrapped her legs around me.

"I was just going to snuggle," I said, stopping in the kitchen to make sure all the burners were off.

She laughed and it vibrated in my chest and lower. "That can come after I do."

"As you wish." I laid her back on the bed and pulled the belt of her robe until it was free.

"You have too many clothes on," she said, tugging the hem of my shirt free.

She deserved to be worshiped, especially after the gift she gave me earlier, and I would show her I loved her... loved every inch of her and not just her body. My heart expanded in my chest with my internal acknowledgment.

"This is for you." I tugged her until her ass was at the end of the bed. Her pussy had been so tight before, I didn't know how she would take both of us, but she did. "Spread your legs for me."

Her knees fell open.

"Good girl. Irresistible." My cock pressed against my pants, longing to be inside her. I resisted that urge. Her center glistened. I swirled my tongue against her clit, taking my time to savor her.

Gemma let a little gasp out.

I dipped my tongue inside her. "Delicious."

Her fingers twined in my hair as she urged my head down.

I sucked down hard on her bundle of nerves. Gemma's hips bucked. I slid a hand up her stomach to her breast and kneaded it in time with my sucking.

"Laurel..." My name was unfettered bliss on her lips.

My dick throbbed to be in her and show her what her

pleasure did to me, but my satisfaction would have to wait. She needed the focus on her. I'd write a sonnet on her body to punctuate my love for her.

I stroked inside her with two fingers and sucked harder. She moaned and writhed under my touch. Her soft walls tightened around my fingers, and her back arched off the bed. Utterances that could have been an ancient language spilled from her mouth, and her pussy contracted. The sight stole my breath. My everything. My undoing. That's what she was to me. She rode the after-shocks out on my fingers as I made languid licks on her. Gemma's breathing slowed, and I withdrew my fingers, sucking her juices off of them.

"Godsdam, that was a sight." I slid up her body, and she pulled me to her, covering my mouth with hers.

"Your turn," she said.

I pulled her into my arms and held her close. I wanted her to understand this was more than my carnal needs. She meant more. "No, the deal was first you come and then we snuggle."

She nestled against my chest. "Are you being nice to me because Cyrus left after he had sex with us?"

Goddesses and gods, I hoped she was joking. My stomach fluttered like a schoolboy, and my heart raced. "No, but I did want to make sure you were okay he left. I'm doing this for you because I...I love you."

She raised up and flattened her hands on my chest, resting her head on top of her fingers. Her curious gaze studied me. "How do you know?"

I was disappointed she didn't say it back, but I

wouldn't pressure her. A ray of sun shot across the room and over the bed. "Because the light shines whenever you are near. There isn't anything I need more than to breathe the same air you do."

She kissed my chest and then found my lips. Her mouth caressed mine in a soft dance. "I taste myself on you."

I licked my lips. "Mmm."

She smiled and her expression turned soft. "I beat up another woman. We can pretend it's because she burned me, but that was only part of the reason. She's hateful and manipulative, and something broke in me when she mentioned my mother. I wanted to beat the hell out of her."

"There is no reason to think of her now or ever. She will never be you. No one will ever be you." I tucked a loose strand of hair behind her ear. "You are the one thing I can't live without."

"I know because you are the one thing I can't live without either." She kissed my forehead and then passionately joined her mouth to mine. She leaned back, and the warmth in her eyes could only be one thing. "I love you," she murmured against my lips.

All my anxiety and fears over where we were going fell away, and I let myself bask in her presence. She was mine, and I was hers. One question lingered unsaid. *Where does Cyrus fit?*

CHAPTER 25

THREE PIECES
GEMMA

Laurel and I were at the table finally eating the meal of potatoes, green vegetables, and roasted chicken. A soft knock sounded from the door, and I looked down at my clothes, thankful Laurel and I had chosen to get dressed after the latest round we spent in bed. He'd had me on all fours, and I relished the way he'd called me a good girl as I came.

A knock rapped again, and Laurel studied me. "Your room."

Oh. Goddesses and gods. My brain was mush after today. "Come in."

Cyrus entered with a glum expression on his handsome face. He looked like he needed consoling, but I wasn't sure that should be me since he left so quickly earlier. I hadn't sensed his approach, and it reminded me I needed to release my barrier. I'd had it down when the three of us were together but plunked it in place out of habit when Laurel and I went to the bedroom earlier. He dropped into the seat next to me.

"What's wrong?"

"The vampires took a unicorn down on the border."

"What?" My heart constricted. I rubbed my chest and scooted my chair closer to him.

"She was on patrol and newly pregnant. The unicorn community is in mourning. She was my cousin. The last child of my aunt who died in the war. She was about fifty years younger than me and Marius."

My heart was gripped by the deep emotion in his voice. I got up and moved behind his chair, wrapping my arms around him. The unicorns seldom spoke of their relations outside of the ones we witnessed. I didn't even know he had this cousin. "I'm so sorry. What was her name?"

"Kelia," he said, his tone mournful. "Named after our great-grandmother."

I rubbed his back. A heaviness settled on my heart for him. "That's a beautiful name. Did the unicorns get the vampire? I can go. You know I'm good at tracking."

I'd never tracked a vampire before, but I'd tracked everything else successfully thanks to my affinity for wind.

He let out a long sigh. "No, that's what I came to talk to you about. I'm going to the scene, but I didn't want to leave without talking about earlier."

My stomach dropped. *Did he not enjoy it the way I did? Did he regret it?* The three of us entwined in our special moment flickered through my mind, but it wasn't the time to think about our love making...no matter how good it had been. Cyrus was hurting. A pang in my gut twisted like I'd eaten a bad piece of meat. He needed support...to know I was here for him.

Laurel reached over the table and put his hand on top of Cyrus's. The gesture was kind and loving. "I'm sorry for your loss. Our soldiers are at your disposal."

"Thank you."

"We can talk about us when you get back," I said. There was more here than any of us had anticipated. We were a unit, but unicorn business would always come first for Cyrus as was their way. I understood that. "But if you want to talk about Keila, I'll always listen."

"No." He took my hand and guided me to my chair. "I want to explain before I leave."

"Cyrus? Are you okay?" He shut me out of our connection, but it wasn't the first time...just the first time since we'd had sex. There were times he would when turmoil occurred in the unicorn world, and the death of a unicorn and a precious unborn foal would certainly do that. I rested a hand on his knee.

"I enjoyed this afternoon," he said, studying us. "I hope you did too."

"Yes, if you couldn't tell," I said.

"I believe we all did." Laurel's eyebrows bunched together.

"And I hope we can move on from there now that we explored our fanciful dalliance." He squeezed the hand I placed on his knee. "It's a distraction none of us can afford and can't happen again."

My heart broke into three pieces—a part for me, a

part for Laurel, and a part for him. The part I held for him shattered. I revered the closeness I'd had with both of them from the experience, but my time alone with Laurel was precious to me in another manner. I loved them both but in different ways. Cyrus saw that. He understood it because of our bond. That must have been why he left and why he didn't want to entertain the idea again.

"I'm sorry for making you feel you had to participate, Cyrus. That was my fantasy, and I never meant for you or any of us to think it wasn't an option. There is always an option to say no."

"You misunderstand. Unicorns do not do things they do not want to. I enjoyed it...probably too much. I care for both of you, but there is a more powerful force at work here. One not even a unicorn can ignore."

"Because Gemma and I are in love." Laurel covered my hand with his similar to how he had for Cyrus.

I glanced at Laurel. My heart warmed at the declaration, but a chunk of it was left cold that Cyrus wasn't part of it.

"Yes, it creates a bond, and I violated that line as a unicorn, a leader, and a bonded."

How could he not see he was a part of us? Of course, it was different because he had to glamour into a faelike form, but he was wanted here. My mind went down erratic paths on what to say to make him understand. "You didn't do anything wrong, Cyrus. That's ridiculous."

He smiled at me. "Always so defiant. Don't let that fire in you ever die, Gemma."

"Why does that sound like a goodbye?" My chest constricted as if my lungs couldn't get enough air.

"I'll be back after we track down the vampire. We can resume your training and see what happens from there."

I swallowed against the hard lump in my throat. Regardless of whether I wanted him to stay or wanted to go with him, he was a unicorn. There was nothing I could do to stop him. First, I lost my siblings and my home. Now, I was losing Cyrus. A fae couldn't interfere with unicorn decisions. I wanted to fight to go with him, but that would cross a line. "Okay."

Our relationship had changed in one passionate moment, and I hoped we could find our way to a future where we were all happy. I wanted to see if the three of us could make it work together, but I'd respect his choice if he didn't see our future the same way.

"Walk me to the edge of the palace grounds?" Cyrus stood and extended a hand each to me and Laurel.

"You never have to ask me to stand by your side," I said. "I'm always there."

CHAPTER 26

CURSE THE TEARS
GEMMA

T wo and a Half Months Later

THE BOND HUMMED in my veins, telling me Cyrus was near. I followed it out to the door we'd entered through the day everything in my world changed. My stomach bottomed out, and I placed one hand on the door for balance and one on my stomach to calm it. I let out a long, deep breath, steadying my nerves, because for the first time since I'd known Cyrus, I was unsure if he wanted to see me. He hadn't reached down the bond once to contact me. While he could have been too far away at times, he certainly wasn't at the moment. He wasn't blocking me, but he wasn't reaching for me either.

I opened the door and hastily nodded to the two guards, scanning the grounds until my gaze landed on his back. He was in his faelike form. I walked toward him, my feet crunching on pebbles. The closer I got to him, the more my vision blurred, and I cursed the tears for distorting my view.

He turned, his mouth curved up in a small smile. I didn't miss the absolute desolation in his eyes. The loss of Keila was so much harder on him than I realized. I couldn't imagine what he must have faced tracking down the vampire responsible.

I wanted to take away every bit of pain from him. He hadn't blocked me, but he had his shields up to prevent me from feeling his agony. I threw my arms around him and pulled him close, pressing my lips to his cheek.

His strong arms enveloped me as he placed a soft kiss on my temple. He didn't hold the embrace too long, and I was certain that had more to do with potential prying eyes than me...at least I hoped it did.

"Come inside." I looped my arm through his.

"I must find Casimir, but I needed to see you first." The vacancy of his eyes filled with something warmer.

"I'm glad you did," I said. "I've missed you...unbearably at times." Leaving the words I wanted to say most unsaid. I loved him. I'd known it before he left, but the time without him here reinforced how much.

With his thumb, he brushed a stray tear from my cheek. "And I you. I got back as soon as I could."

"Go take care of your business with Casimir, so we can properly catch up. Laurel will be happy to see you, too. He's out in the forest gathering herbs and plants." I patted his arm, wanting to do so much more.

He released my arm. "I missed you both. I'll come to see you shortly."

Our gazes locked, and I saw a smoldering fire staring back at me. Desire unleashed down our bond like a broken dam. My lower belly clenched.

Cyrus hesitated. Then, the intense yearning was gone, ripped away, and I knew he'd closed down the bond. His eyes were once again vacant. He opened his mouth and closed it before turning toward the gate.

"I'll see you soon." A conversation would be had later. I'd sensed his confusion in the bond before he shut it off. That was my fault, and I would do my best to fix it.

He grunted out an indecipherable response.

I watched him walk toward the area of the city where the unicorns had built a row of homes until he disappeared down the street. My heart never stopped hurting to see him leave.

CHAPTER 27

BROKEN PROMISE

GEMMA

The new paint scent wafted around me in nauseating fashion. I breathed out through my mouth. When Laurel had suggested we remodel a room in the far side of the royal wing, I jumped at the opportunity. I was over hearing Rain tease me and my mate about how active our sexual habits were. Laurel and I needed privacy. Save the blue and silver royal crest in the living room, he and I had chosen light natural colors.

"Are you okay? You look a little...green," Laurel said.

I smiled and touched his forearm. "I'm fine. The paint odor is just strong."

He inhaled. "I like the smell."

I laughed. "Of course you do." I blew out another breath. "The rest of the furniture, including our bed, is supposed to be here tomorrow."

Laurel wrapped his arms around my waist and pulled me close. "I, for one, cannot wait to break that particular piece of furniture in."

I glanced around him at the large overstuffed L-shaped couch he'd bent me over yesterday. He'd only paused when I told him not to stain the alabaster fabric. "You seemed to enjoy the sofa."

The oval dark wood coffee and end tables arrived with the shearling rug not long after we finished, and I was concerned the fae guards delivering them might know what we'd been doing a few minutes before.

He nuzzled his nose against mine. "If you haven't noticed, I'll take you anywhere I can have you."

My bond with Cyrus, nearly silent since his return, flared to life with fear and random thoughts. He was searching for me...for us. A shudder slammed through me. My knees buckled from the intensity of the terror Cyrus felt. He was getting closer.

"What—"

The door opened and banged against the wall. I knew it was my bonded from our connection, but Laurel shoved me behind him. I ducked under his arm, my senses returning.

"Cyrus?" Laurel asked, his tone confused.

"What's wrong?" I asked, taking in how pale Cyrus was. "Are you hurt?"

He was breathing hard, something I'd never seen him do. When he moved toward me and Laurel, he looked us over as if needing confirmation my mate and I were okay.

"You're scaring me. What's going on?"

He raised a hand as if to touch me, but dropped it. "I'm sorry. We got word that your father was glimpsed in the city, and then there was an attack on the front. I was afraid he'd found you and the skirmish at the vampire border was a distraction to draw Rain there."

Shock shattered my fear. My father was spotted here? Why?

"My brother is at the front," Laurel said. "How bad is the attack?"

"Still going," Cyrus said.

A knot formed in my stomach. "We should go help."

"I need to go, but this isn't your battle." My mate brushed his fingers against my cheek. "I'd rather know you are safe."

"You're not going to sideline me, Laurel. This is my family and my people now." The only thing keeping me from telling him off was the urgency of the situation and that I knew he was worried about his brother. I would be if it was Ari.

He gave me a sad smile. "You're right."

"Perhaps grab some weapons and then vanyshen there," Cyrus said, sounding resigned.

"Are you going too?" Laurel asked him.

"Of course."

***

Loaded down with every weapon we could fit, I was glad I'd been in my training clothes, so at least I was going into the fight in pants.

"Have you ever vanyshened with a unicorn?" Cyrus asked, raising an eyebrow at Laurel.

"Not a unicorn but a horse many times. That's basically the same thing."

Cyrus turned to face him, shifting into his faelike form and crossing his arms. "No, it's not at all."

"Can we settle that argument later?" I asked.

Laurel held his hands out to both me and Cyrus. I slipped mine into my mate's. Cyrus hesitated but took Laurel's hand. Even though we were going into danger, I was excited every time we vanyshened. Wind whipped around us as the colors swirled and sparkled in brilliancy unseen otherwise. As the gleaming light winked away to normal, I noticed how dark the sky was. Laurel guided us to an easy landing, and the sound of the realm returned.

Metal clinks pounded through the air with shouts and fleshy sounds. The battle was in full swing. I pulled the sword at my back free. To my left, Cyrus had returned to his natural form. To my right, Laurel retrieved his sword and took his fighting stance. In front of us were warriors dressed in blue and silver uniforms like some of the palace guards. There were so many of them that it took me a moment to register how many vampires were on the other side of them. *Fuck.* Adrenaline chased away my fear. "I don't see your brother?"

"He's probably looking for a high place where he can get the advantage."

I sent my mate a sidelong glance. "He's hiding?"

"No." Laurel grinned. "You'll see when the battle ends. Ready?"

"Ready," I responded.

"I'm here to kill vampires," Cyrus said, running ahead of us. He kicked up black dirt with his hooves, and I noticed the ground had already been stained red with blood. Our soldiers had pushed the vampires back at some point, but it looked like the vampires had gained most of the ground back.

I must be crazy, because I should be afraid. My blood pumped through my veins, and I was eager for the fight.

Laurel nodded, and we both took off at a clipped pace. Side-by-side, we entered the fight. Laurel cut through the mass of vampires and disappeared. A vampire came straight at me, and I dropped into the low position, slicing through her middle with my sword. The spine was the only resistance I met. I'd never been in a battle like this, and the sounds overwhelmed me. I gazed around at the conflict. Dark vampire blood spattered across my clothes where a fae soldier relieved the male of his arms. The brutal action was unnecessary, but I'd heard stories of worse during the Great War.

A hiss skated over my skin. *Too close.* I spun around. My naive distraction cost me my momentum. Vampires closed the ring they had formed around me. There was no opening. I had to fight my way out.

Between two of the vampires, I caught sight of Laurel. His gaze, filled with fear, met mine. He tried to cut through vampires, but there were too many. Twice as many vampires as were surrounding me descended on him, and I could no longer see him.

Stay alive. I'm on my way. Cyrus sent down our bond.

No. Go save Laurel. Please. I'm fine.

Gemma...

Promise me you'll get him safe first, Cyrus.

A long pause made me think he had ignored me. *I promise.*

The vampires tightened their ranks, closing in around me. I caught a glimpse of Laurel. He thrashed against the horde pulling him to the ground—fangs sunk in his arms, his legs, his neck. Though I heard no noises over the thunder of the battle, his mouth opened in a scream.

Cyrus. Save my mate. Get him out of here.

I am. Then I'm coming back for you.

A vampire exploded into pieces, and I relaxed a fraction. Cyrus had gotten to Laurel in time. They would make it out...even if I didn't. I swung my sword, summoning my wind magic to guide my sword. The metal sliced clean through the necks of two vampires. The remaining blood-suckers came forward, just out of reach.

Wind rushed around me, but it wasn't my doing. The vampires struggled to keep their ground. A barrel flew over, followed by a limb. *What the fuck.* I struggled to turn and saw a funnel-shaped cloud. It swirled in circles, gaining momentum and destroying everything in its path.

Gemma?

Are you seeing this—

Get out of there.

The vampires fared better against the wind than I did. I dropped to the ground, and they hovered over me. I thought of my mother and her sacrifice...of my sister and brother who would suffer grief again. *I'm sorry.* I closed my eyes, preparing for the pain to come. If I was going to die, it would be with sweet memories. I replayed the way I awakened during the bonding ceremony with Cyrus and dancing with Laurel. Then, my mind took over showing me the night Cyrus, Laurel, and I made love. Let that be the last thing I remember.

I love you. The words drifted to my bonded. *Tell him I love him too.*

Where are you? I don't see you. Fuck, Gemma. You need to get out of there.

It's too late. I closed off the bond the way he'd taught me.

A vampire's head jerked up, eyes wide. Lightning speared him through the head. He tumbled backward, landing with a thud. *Fucking lightning. Too bad it didn't deter the others.* I planted the heel of my boot in the chest of the closest one. He flew back. A bolt of lightning struck his chest, knocking him straight into the funnel. Bright streaks flashed around me. The ground rumbled, making it impossible to stand. I covered my eyes and huddled down. Wind whipped around me, and everything went quiet like when I was in the bubble with Persephone...only I hadn't made one. I peeked out from under my arm. All I could see was bright, blinding light. I tried to stand and run, but my feet were swept out from under me. When I landed, the hit knocked the air from my lungs. My head bashed into something hard. Pain splintered through my skull and my vision tunneled into darkness.

***

I blinked, and light filled the space around me. Air caught in my lungs. Was I still on the battlefield? I inhaled deeply and smelled the delicate scent of a moonflower.

"She's awake," Cyrus said, his voice anguished.

My vision cleared, and I focused on the foot of the bed. *My bed.* Cyrus stood at the end with one knee on the dove grey settee. Laurel, beside him, looked healthy and not like vampires had bitten him a dozen times. How long had I been out?

"What happened?" My voice sounded rough and not like my own.

"Do you remember the battle?" Laurel asked, handing me a cup of tea and easing onto the bed beside me.

I sat up, and Laurel adjusted the fluffy pillows against the upholstered headboard behind me. All of the furniture was in place. The darker grey bedside stands. The dresser, the same color as the settee, was placed in the exact spot we'd discussed. Two darker gray chairs and a matching ottoman were by the floor-to-ceiling windows where I'd imagined reading some of the romance novels I'd found in the library. Even the flower arrangement I'd imagined was on the beverage table between the chairs. I'd missed it all.

"Yes, I recall everything up until I was knocked down and hit my head." I gestured between them. "One of you fill me in on the rest. Starting with how long I've been out."

"You slept for a day and a half. We think it was a trauma response because..." My mate paused and looked at my bonded.

"This can't leave the room," Cyrus said.

Laurel pressed his lips into a grim smile and nodded his head.

"I healed you both. No one can know. I've broken many promises, but using certain unicorn magic is forbidden outside of the unicorn collective. To extend the life of a fae is considered tampering with fate."

"Cyrus," I whispered, setting the cup on the marble coaster atop the side table.

Laurel took my hand and squeezed. "We owe him our silence."

"I've no doubt,' I said to Laurel and studied Cyrus. His black eyes were wells of unreadable emotions. I patted the comforter on the open side of the bed. "Sit, Cyrus."

He studied me, his face softening, and took the offered place.

"Thank you." I leaned over and kissed his cheek. "But what about unicorn business always coming first? What will happen if someone saw what you did?"

"My brother will be forced to punish me."

I sat straight up, ignoring the protests from my limbs. "Punish you? How?"

Cyrus turned his gaze toward the doorway. "Marius could banish me, or if my offense is deemed to be egregious, he could order death."

"We'll have to make sure no one finds out," Laurel said matter-of-factly.

"It will be our secret," I said, pulling each of their hands into my lap. "A broken promise will bind us forever."

CHAPTER 28

SACRIFICES
GEMMA

I reclined on the healer's examination table pondering the events of the two weeks since Cyrus returned and the vampire battle. Cyrus had given few details of the time hunting Keila's killer but I was certain the vampire's end involved a painful death from a unicorn horn. Then again, that might have been too swift a death. Either way, Cyrus hadn't discussed it other than to say he'd finished the mission. He'd stayed at a distance since the day I'd woken from the battle, and I didn't push him. I suspected he was still dealing with the grief from losing his cousin. The difficulty of grief was something I understood. I wouldn't force my comfort on him to appease my own need to be close to him. He seemed to drift further and further away though, and that worried me.

I'd been working with Laurel daily on my magic in a training facility with safeguards to make sure I didn't bring down the city. The center had been designed to make sure no one was hurt and no buildings were destroyed. Laurel even taught me how to vanyshen, a way to travel between locations in seconds—something that had been blocked in the prison kingdom and apparently a magic trait not all fae had. Only the most powerful could do it, and I could. It was the first time I'd realized Ari wasn't the only daughter who had inherited some of my mother's talents. After the first time I was able to travel a distance, I visited Mother's statue. The sun stood high in the sky when I knelt before her likeness with tears in my eyes. I placed a wreath of moonflowers at the base. Only a few people had been around, and they gave me space. I didn't linger, not wanting to draw attention. The words I'd spoken as I gazed at her face were the same ones I'd wished I could have told her when she was alive. *Thank you, Mother. Not just for the sacrifice you gave our empire, but for telling me to look for you in the forest.* I placed my hand on the base. *Thank you for your gifts. All the good I do here will be in your name.*

My training sessions with Cyrus resumed a few days after the battle, and they had been brutal. He pushed me in both magic and physical combat. He told me I needed to be better prepared for future battles. I trusted him. There were moments when we were close for certain moves, I thought he might kiss me. He never did, no matter how much I willed it. Occasionally, his hand would brush over mine or over my hip, and I'd swear his eyes would smolder. Not once did he act on it if he was longing for me the way I was for him.

The day Cyrus returned, he embraced me like he'd

missed me, and I'd certainly missed him. The smile on his face played on repeat in my mind, because I hadn't seen many in the last few weeks. The attraction was still there for me, and Laurel had said it was for him. Laurel didn't push Cyrus either, giving him the time to sort through it in his own time. Although he had watched TV and taken some meals with us, there hadn't been any other intimate engagements. A new normal settled over us. If Cyrus was okay with it, I was too as long as he was here. Pressuring him to do something he was against or that compromised his beliefs wasn't a topic I would pursue...even if my heart was screaming to love him.

I'd fainted—third time in a month. That's why we were in the healer's center. While Laurel was in meetings, Cyrus and I had been training when the dizziness hit me. Cyrus caught me before I hit the ground and carried me to the infirmary.

"Did the doctor say which tests they were running this time?" I asked Cyrus, remembering to use the correct term since they didn't call them healers here any longer.

Concern creased his face. "No. Is your body telling you something is wrong? I can ask them to check if it is."

I shook my head. "I feel fine. I've been a little tired, but I'm sure it's just using too much power at once. I'm still learning my limits. We've been pushing pretty hard too."

"True. I can see the stress on Laurel's face. He said Rain was heading to the front again tomorrow."

"Please don't tell him I fainted again. He doesn't need the extra drama right now."

Cyrus averted his eyes.

"You told him already?"

"I sent word to him. Yes."

"Ugh." I slammed my head back into the pillow. "He's going to think he has to wait on my every whim."

Cyrus chuckled. It was the first real laugh I'd heard out of him since he'd been back. A warmth like a hug drifted across our bond. "Most women would welcome that from their partner."

I smiled at him. "I think we've established I'm not like most fae women." I covered my eyes with my arm. "I don't know what to do with myself here, Cyrus."

He gently pulled my arm away from my face. "Maybe it's time you went out into the city to spend time with your people."

"I'd like that. There's an animal rehabilitation center. I think I could do good there. There's a school for gifted wind wielders—The King Veran School for Mastering the Art of Wind. Mother always said my affinity for wind was there from the womb."

"You should do that." He sat in the chair by the bed and took my hand. While he hadn't avoided touching me in training, he hadn't attempted to hold my hand since before his cousin had been murdered.

Tears pricked my eyes, and it made me feel like an idiot for being so sniveling. "Thank you."

"I did nothing but remind you of who you are—the badass princess who can target a grasshopper or an army with her wind magic."

The tears in my eyes nearly spilled over, and I had to

blink them back. "I don't know why I'm getting all weepy. You know I don't usually cry."

The door opened, and he released my hand. A doctor, the same one who had checked me out last time, entered the room.

"How are you feeling, Gemma?" Doctor Brychan asked.

"I feel fine. Do we know what's wrong with me?"

"Nothing is wrong with you." He smiled and patted my foot.

"I don't understand. Why do I keep fainting? Am I pushing myself too hard? Am I just tired?"

"Yes, and that's probably going to keep happening for a few months." He glanced at Cyrus. "Do you want this news alone?"

"I knew it," Cyrus whispered under his breath.

"Just tell me," I said.

Doctor Brychan's smile grew. He passed me a piece of paper. "I ran one test we hadn't run the last two times. You're pregnant, Gemma. About ten to twelve or so weeks is where you look to be. We can do more precise testing when you're ready."

"Close your mouth," Cyrus muttered.

I trembled. Disbelief and adrenaline coursed through my veins."But I take the monthly contraception and so does Laurel. We haven't missed a dose."

"It's not infallible. Sometimes the Fates decide for us."

The idea someone else decided for me pissed me off, but Laurel and I had a lot of sex too. It shouldn't be the shock it was.

"If you don't want the pregnancy, there are op— "

I held up my hand. My shock turned to happiness. Laurel and I had created a life. "No, the baby is wanted. I just hadn't expected it so soon."

"Do you have any questions for me?"

"No, but I'm sure I will."

"I'll prepare a prenatal plan and will meet with you next week if that works."

"Yes," I said. "Thank you."

"You can leave whenever you are ready. If you or Laurel have any questions, I'm available anytime." He paused at the door. "Congratulations."

I smiled at him and watched the door shut. Then, I stared at the test results. Ten to twelve weeks or so. If I was twelve weeks or longer— that was around the time Laurel and I first slept together, but also, the same week the three of us were together.

"Cyrus, what are the possibilities here? Could this be our baby?" Tears burned my eyes again. I felt guilty for hoping it wasn't. I didn't want to tie him to us when he seemed to have made a firm decision on our boundaries, and I wasn't sure how Laurel would feel if the baby wasn't his.

"This is why it is forbidden, Gemma." Cyrus cupped my face with very human hands. "A half-elf and half-unicorn would not survive even this long. Your baby is very much entirely you and Laurel, as it should be. As it should always have been."

Tears spilled over my eyes and burned down my cheeks. "I don't want you to leave."

He swiped away the dampness with his thumbs. "We

were never meant to be. Two legs and two feet aren't natural for me. I belong on four legs and the ability to run with such. Laurel is your mate, and your daughter will be magnificent like her mother and grandmother."

"Daughter?" I choked out between sobs.

"Yes, she will come into this world like your mother did."

"But my mother almost died when she was born." I studied his face. A single golden tear slid from the corner of his eye. I reached up to catch it and held my hand out for him. "You know how valuable these are and probably more in this place."

His eyes closed in a slow blink. "It is my gift to you, and you will know when to use it."

I stood to look for a container to hold the tear. "Please don't leave. We'll figure out a way. We won't sleep together anymore."

He stepped back from me. "You know we can't go back to being a guardian and his bonded charge. It's been a struggle even in training since I've been back. The line has been blurred for more than a year now. Our time together only sealed that. I must go."

I scrambled around the infirmary for a vial to put the tear in. "I don't want you to..." The words evaporated into thin air. Cyrus wasn't in the room any longer.

Cyrus? I called to our bond. The bond was intact, but he didn't respond. *Please don't do this.*

If ever there is a time you need me, truly need my help, I promise I will be there. Until then, live strong and long with

Laurel and your daughter. He was gone like a door had closed. He'd shut me out.

I stared down at the test results, and the gold tear in the vial next to them. Resting my hand on my belly, I focused my thoughts on my daughter. *You will live, my little girl. I promise you that. Even if we must leave this kingdom, you will have the life you deserve.*

Cyrus had said the baby would arrive like my mother. She told the healers of the circumstances of her birth when she had Ari. They'd been concerned Ari was breech, but she wasn't. She was in distress, and I'd always believed she'd been saved by the grace of Nyx. Mother's birth, by her own account, had been near death. Her umbilical cord had been wrapped around her throat and cut off her air. She said she had been blue. *Was that the destiny of my daughter? If so, being here is the safest place with the modern technology and gifted healers.*

First things first. I had to share the news with Laurel that I was having his child. The doors opened, and he appeared in the entrance as if I'd summoned him.

"I was on my way here when Cyrus found me. He told me he was leaving. I came to see if you were okay." His words came out in a worried rush. He took slow, careful steps toward me.

"Did he tell you?"

Concern deepened in lines across his face. "Just that he was leaving. Is there something else?"

I stifled a sob.

He reached for me with a cautious touch, and I let him pull me to his chest, the results paper in one hand and the vial in the other. Laurel stroked my back. "I know how much he means to you."

"He does and he always will. You are my mate and the father of my child." I whispered against his ear.

"What?" He pulled back and studied my face. Confusion flittered over his features.

"I'm pregnant with your child. My mate's child."

"We're pregnant?" His slow smile grew to a broad display of happiness.

I nodded. "According to this test, maybe even from the very first time."

He pressed his lips to my forehead. "I love you, Gemma." His mouth found mine and devoured it. When he pulled back, his eyes dazzled like the brightest gemstone. "I knew we were mates when I saw you in the forest, but I thought it might have been that damn forest playing tricks on me."

"And now?"

"I know it was all you." He grinned.

"You are so full of yourself."

He rubbed his hand over my stomach. "And you are full of me."

I laughed and swatted his shoulder. "She's part of both of us."

"It's a girl?"

"That was Cyrus's parting gift. He said we're having a little girl."

Laurel covered his mouth. He was clearly in shock, and I wanted to laugh but I was afraid he was going to pass out.

"Are you okay?"

"I'm going to be a dad. We're going to be parents." His tone was so joyful.

"Are you happy about it?"

He picked me up and wrapped my arms around his neck. He spun me around and set me down. "I'm beyond happy. Whatever is a thousand times that. But I'm worried about something else."

The love radiating off him lightened my heart. Any anxiety I had disappeared. My happiness swelled to replace my nervousness."Look, Laurel, Cyrus and I have known each other for a long time, but you are my mate. You will always come first." I rubbed my belly. "Except for this little one, and I hope you're okay with coming second to her."

"Of course, I am." He kissed me again. "I had something planned for tonight, and now, I'm worried you will think this news influenced me, but it didn't. I've been working on it all week."

CHAPTER 29
THE FLOWERS
LAUREL

I knelt on one knee in front of Gemma as was the custom. The floral scent from all the flowers I had delivered filled the music room. She'd come here to play when she wasn't with me or training with Cyrus. I'd found her here many times and even made love to her on top of the piano more than once. When I decided to propose, this was the place that spoke to me most as a part of her. While our start had been anything but what a normal courtship would have been, she was my mate, and I loved her with every ounce of my power. So why hadn't she just said yes? Instead, we were debating, and I was still on my knee. "I know we haven't had a traditional relationship the past few months, but I want to spend the rest of my eternity with you here and beyond."

"Don't you think we should wait? Until after our daughter is born?"

I stood then and brushed her hair back over her shoulders. "What's really bothering you? Are you unsure if you love me? If I'm your mate?"

She winced at the last question. So, that was it.

"Mate sounds like we didn't have a say in it. That we didn't have a choice to love each other, and I don't want you to ever feel like you don't have a choice to be with me." Her forehead bunched up.

"Gemma." I cupped her face in my hands. "I loved you before I knew you were my mate, and I'd love you even if you weren't. The brightest rays of the sun dim in your presence. When I enter a room you occupy, I only see you. There is nothing I want more than to spend all our time together in bed showing you in every way how much you mean to me."

A smile spread across her face as a few tears leaked from the corners of her eyes. "Someone will have to leave the bed to change diapers and feed our daughter."

"I think we can share those tasks." I brushed my lips across her forehead, loving away her tension. "So, Gemma, love of my fae heart, will you join your life with mine?"

She nodded. "Yes, of course I will."

Air swooshed around us and colors swirled up, surrounding us with flowers. *My mate's magic.* Unlike the funnels from my brother's power, Gemma created a gentle protective space. I watched in fascination. Petals drifted down like a gentle cascading rain over us. *Magnificent.* I captured her mouth with mine in a gentle caress. Love radiated between us and flowed over me like a waterfall.

I plucked a petal from Gemma's hair and hugged her

to me. Relief spread through every part of my body that she'd agreed to marry me. "Please don't ever make me worry like that again."

CHAPTER 30
THE TEAR
GEMMA

Six months later

The cramps intensified as soon as my water broke. Blood streamed down my leg, and I knew this was the moment Cyrus warned me of months earlier. My mate's face was white like he was about to pass out.

"If we don't do something now, she's not going to survive, Laurel." Sweat rolled down my face. He scooped me up and put me in the bed in the med ward.

"Doctor Brychan is on his way."

"The unicorn tear Cyrus gave me. It's in my top drawer. He knew. That's why he gave it to me." I gritted my teeth to get the words out. Unsure exactly how to use the tear, I had faith the knowledge would reveal itself. Cyrus wouldn't have left us if it wasn't the case. I tried to focus between the sharp stabs of pain.

"I'm not leaving you to get it."

"You can vanyshen there and back in seconds. I'll be fine, but our daughter won't." I squinted my eyes shut as another contraction bore down. I huffed out a breath as it eased. "Go now."

"We can't vanyshen in the palace." His face went paler. He was in shock or something and needed to move.

"Then run. Now. We need it." He disappeared in a breeze. Tears burned my eyes. We were not going to lose her. The seconds ticked by, and I wondered if he was going to make it back in time to save our baby girl. *Goddesses and gods, please. I beg you. Help us save her.*

A hand gripped my shoulder. I glanced at it, and no one was touching me. A calm came over me, starting in my mind and working down my neck. The soothing sensation spread to my limbs. Was this their answer? Were they telling me she was going to live?

The doctor and assistants prepped me for the procedure he'd talked us through last week. Cyrus...I could reach for him.

Papers flew off the table as my mate returned. "I've got it."

I let out a slow breath.

Doctor Brychan patted my foot like he had the day he told me I was pregnant. "We're going to start the procedure right away. You'll be holding your baby girl in moments."

I didn't argue with him. Laurel had the tear. I was convinced the goddesses and gods had given me their reassurance. The procedure was the best chance our little girl had.

"Aagh." The pain spiked like a poker in my gut. "She wants out."

"Magic isn't working. We need to open Gemma up and retrieve the baby," the doctor explained to Laurel.

I clutched my mate's hand. "Promise me you will use the tear on her. Not me. No matter what happens. You promise me."

Tears formed in his eyes. He knew what I was asking, but he hesitated. "I love you, Gemma. With my magic, I bind this promise to do what it takes to save you both, but your bonded's tear is yours to decide and will be for our daughter alone."

I closed my eyes and another contraction hit like fire and fury. A monitor went wild with alarms.

"It's the baby's heart rate," one of the doctors said. "We need to get the baby out now or we're going to lose them both."

Laurel

THE BABY WAS blue as the doctor removed the cord from her neck. They suctioned her mouth, but nothing happened. Silence. No cries. I pushed the staff away and pulled the tear from my pocket, pouring it on my daughter's chest. A bright light engulfed her and appeared to be absorbed into her tiny body. I pressed my hand and sent my healing magic into her. Nothing happened. I sent another dose of my power into her, searching for Cyrus's tear and the energy of it, latching onto that ancient gift and willing it to her heart. A cry so loud they probably heard it across the empire erupted from her tiny lungs.

I wept as I picked her up and wrapped a blanket around her. She was alive. Cyrus had saved her, and he wasn't even here. "Hello, beautiful. You look just like your mommy. Do you want to meet her?"

My daughter's life force was bright like the sunlight the day I told Gemma I loved her. I turned back to where the doctors were sewing Gemma up. She was watching me with our daughter. Tears spilled down her cheeks. My mate had given me this gift. I was a father.

"We are parents." I held our daughter where her mother could get a good look.

She touched our child's face with her finger. "Hi, baby girl." Gemma looked up at me with so much emotion I couldn't decipher it. "I know we hadn't settled on a name before she made her appearance, but I'd like to name her after my mother."

I smiled and took in our little fighter, and that's what she was. Her entrance wasn't easy, but she was here. "I think there is no name more perfect for her."

Gemma kissed our baby's forehead. "Hello, Daphina, my beautiful daughter."

Overwhelming joy filled my heart. I had a family, and I didn't think that would ever come to be. Yet, here she was. My perfect daughter and her incredible mother. "You'll be Phina to me. Daphina is a big name you'll need to grow into."

My daughter's mouth formed an O, and I wondered if she was telling me I was too much already.

"I wish my sister was here to meet you, Phina," Gemma said, her tears falling faster. "She will know you one day, though, and I know she will love you as much as I do."

"Do you want me to put her on your chest?"

"Yes," Gemma said.

Phina nestled against Gemma. "Perfection."

MY BROTHER ENTERED our suites and clapped me on the shoulder, gazing down at my daughter like she was the sun. She already had her uncle wrapped around her little finger. "She's beautiful. Thank goodness she took after Gemma."

"Fuck off, Rain," I said, chuckling. I was glad she looked like my mate and not me too.

Gemma came in with a bottle. "Hi, Rain." She looked at me and smiled at our daughter while holding a bottle. "These are the best inventions."

"Because you get some freedom?" Rain asked.

"No, because your brother gets to experience what it's like to feed our daughter. They get to share that moment."

My brother's face softened. Maybe love was in the future for him. "Can I try?"

His request surprised me, but I liked the idea of my brother seeing what it was like to have a real family. "Go sit in the big chair."

Rain sat in the rocking chair and held his arms out.

"You do know how to hold a baby, don't you?" I asked.

He stared at me but didn't say anything.

"See how I'm cradling her with this arm and supporting her head? You must make sure you do that."

Gemma chuckled. "Put her in his arms. He's not going to hurt her."

I placed Phina in his arms and adjusted him. He held her securely, but my brother hadn't spent any time around babies. Rain looked at her the way I felt—like she hung the moon. She was going to have her father and her uncle wrapped around her finger.

My mate patted my shoulder and handed me the bottle. "He's got her."

"You want to hold the bottle like this." I showed him the angle. "That keeps the milk in the end, so she doesn't suck in a lot of air."

"Brother, I've got it." He took the bottle from me. "You're so hungry. Are they starving my little niece?" Rain asked as he watched her, and I knew he would do anything to protect her just like I would. She was going to have an army to watch over her.

"I think we found our future babysitter." Gemma wrapped her arms around my waist. I slung mine around her shoulders.

"You mean her only babysitter," Rain said, smiling. "I'm not letting anyone near my niece."

I laughed. "Let's see how you do with a dirty diaper first. Then we can decide if you qualify for babysitting duty."

Gemma arched a brow. She'd been sitting in on the

meetings for Rain until she had Phina. "Don't you have a meeting with advisors in fifteen minutes?"

"They just want to lecture me about picking a wife, so I can finally be crowned." My brother gave zero fucks about being forced into an arranged marriage. He'd avoided those discussions since he had taken the throne.

"What?" Gemma asked. "I'd wondered why you were still referred to as prince instead of king."

"There is some old fae law that the coronation can't take place until he's married."

"That's stupid," Gemma said. "Why don't you change it?

"Only the king can change that law," Rain said. "Which I am not yet."

Gemma laughed and shook her head. "What in the world?"

"You thought this place was so much more evolved than your prison kingdom, but even some things here are ancient customs that still need to change. That is work you could help with, Gemma." Rain studied my wife as if he were gauging his next move, and that made me uncomfortable. "I'd like to name you the head of a committee of modernization. We'll want to preserve our history and some traditions, but we need a fresh perspective on how to move forward with our tech and magic."

"Why me? I grew up without all this technology and am learning it myself."

"Precisely why it should be you. I think you can bring an outlook that will help us reprioritize our efforts to the most important things." He held up the empty bottle.

I took it from him and put a cloth on his shoulder. "Lift her to your shoulder and gently but firmly pat her back."

Rain positioned our daughter as I instructed while he waited for Gemma's response. My mate looked stunned, but I thought she was perfect for the position, especially with her helpful soul.

"You can say no," I said to her. "You are not obligated to do any of this."

"I don't want to give up teaching the children with a wind magic affinity like mine. I don't want this appointment if it will interfere with teaching them."

"The kids at the school have grown attached to you over the past few months." I smiled, knowing how much her time volunteering at the school has meant to her. "But I think you could do both if you want."

I looked at Phina. I wanted her to know the realm had no limits for her—she could be and do anything she wanted, just like her mother.

Gemma squeezed my hand and gave a single nod toward Rain. "I'll do it."

Rain grinned. "Welcome to the team." Phina burped. He rubbed her back. "Your turn will have to wait a couple of decades, sweet girl."

I slid my arm around Gemma's waist and hugged her to my side. She wrapped her arms around my midsection. This was our family, but I knew she felt incomplete without her siblings here. Part of me sensed a piece of us missing, too, and maybe one day Cyrus would return and complete our family. I couldn't blame him if he didn't, but I sure would like him to meet the daughter he helped bring into this world with his tear—Princess Daphina Cyra Arianna. Gemma said her sister would hate the long name but love the gesture, and I wondered if Cyrus would appreciate we gave our daughter the feminine version of his. The priority had to be her sister because what neither Rain nor I told her was that Arianna was the key to so much more. Casimir was certain Arianna inherited General Daphina's powers—all of them and more. We would free my mate's siblings, the citizens trapped there, and all the others in that cursed kingdom across the forest, even if we had to do it one at a time.

CHAPTER 31

FAMILY

GEMMA

F*our years later*

THE NEWS ARRIVED through Rain's bonded unicorn, Casimir. The magic was failing in the prison world, and the vampires were getting closer each day. The prison would drain Ari's magic just like it had Mother's. My sister's power had already been impacted. Casimir relayed that Ari could hardly use it because when she did, it made her sick. It would only get worse for my sister the longer we waited. The only way she would be safe was to get her away from our prison home. She and Drew both.

"Did Casimir tell you anything else? Did she mention Drew at all?"

Rain gave a grim shake of his head. "No, she didn't say his name, but the communication was brief."

I looked up into my mate's eyes and saw the worry he carried for my family he'd never met. "They're going to be all right, aren't they?"

He wrapped his fingers around my shoulder and pulled me close. "Nothing is going to happen to them."

"I have to go get her. I can't leave Ari to die there." Or worse than death at my father's hands. If he broke free of the confines of that prison, his memories would return. He'd be the tyrant who nearly handed our people to the nosferatu two hundred years ago. Neither Ari nor Drew would be safe there. I wouldn't let my father mistreat my siblings. I was the eldest, and it was my responsibility to make sure that nothing harmed them.

"While we might be able to sneak you in, you'd be recognized," Laurel said. "Your father thinks you have been brainwashed here, so he'd probably confine you if he caught you on that side of the forest."

"I can't just leave her there—with our father. She'll be drained like our mother if the vampires don't get there first. And my little brother..."

"I'll go," Laurel said.

I shook my head. He was close to a breakthrough. "You can't. You have too much research at stake with the unicorns."

"Neither of you can go. You have my niece to take care of, and she needs both of her parents to look after her precocious cuteness." Rain patted my back. "It has to be me. I'm the only one who can make them believe I'm from the prison kingdom."

"Because of your gift," Laurel said. I studied my mate's

brother. His mouth, set in a firm line, aligned with his decision.

Rain nodded. He hated using the changeling power, but it didn't really change him. It only altered what other people saw.

"But weren't you scheduled for another trip to the front?" I asked. He went when his power was needed or there had been a substantial attack. The latter happened more and more often, which meant the vampire forces were testing us as they tried to find their way to my father.

"I'll figure it out. We'll incorporate it into the plan." Rain sounded confident, but it didn't calm the nerves roiling in my stomach.

"Whose identity can you use?" Laurel asked, pinning me to his side. It was a good thing because I wasn't sure I could stand on my own.

"The Prince of Agonburg was injured during a clash with the vampire soldiers. He hasn't been at court since, and we share a first name, which will make it easier."

"I knew his brother, but he was older. He was pretty talented and smug. I'm not sure you can pull that off."

Rain smirked. "I can be quite charming."

He was damn convincing. "Go get my sister, Rain. Get her out of there now before the vampires break my father out of the spell."

He nodded. "Work on a plan with your team on how to help the people of the prison world acclimate to life here. We'll need to make sure the transition is as easy as possible for them. They have sacrificed for our way of life here. Don't tell them I'm going. Leave that out."

"I understand discretion, Rain." I inhaled and calmed my attitude. He was rescuing my siblings for me, his brother's mate, but keeping my father imprisoned kept our empire safe too. "I'll meet with my committee tomorrow, and we'll have a plan in place by the time you get back."

"There are some fae I think will be helpful with the task, so I'll text you those names before I leave."

"Thank you, Rain." I hugged him.

He pulled back and smiled. "This is what family does, Gemma. This is what your mother would have done."

My heart swelled at the realization of how my household had changed and grown. It wasn't perfect, but I knew he was right—Mother would have done everything she could to make our family whole again. I blinked back tears. *Nyx, guide him.*

My siblings were coming...home.

Ready for more? Read Cyrus's book next, and if you haven't read Ari's first book, Crown of Night and Rain, start there.

CRAVING MORE PASSION AND MAGIC?

The magic you've experienced in these pages is just the beginning of the Empire of Curses and Dreams world. Join my newsletter family for exclusive content—from deleted scenes to sneak peeks of upcoming releases. I share writing updates, behind-the-scenes views, and magical surprises with my most devoted readers first. Let's continue this journey together

Acknowledgments

To my editors, Dawn and Lisa, thank you for making me a better writer with every book, and especially for being supportive when I want to try something new with my storytelling. Your honesty is so valuable in making this series the best it can be.

To my cover designer, Laura, I still can't believe where we started from to where we ended for this beautiful cover. It depicts elements of the story I never expected we could do. That is because of your incredible talent!

To my sister and my nieces, thank you for being there on all the twists and turns of my writing journey, whether that's a new partnership or joining me for a signing.

To my friend, Lizzie, thank you for supporting me, making me laugh, being an extra set of eyes, and reminding me to ignore the impostor syndrome.

To my beta readers, ARC readers, and fans, your acceptance of this series and excitement for this book and the others coming in the series have been what I dreamed of as a writer. Thank you!

ABOUT THE AUTHOR

Susan Person is an award-winning author of fantasy and dark paranormal romance. After years in the business world, she returned to college to pursue a degree in anthropology and graduated in 2021. Susan enjoys meeting writers and readers alike at conferences and events. She knew at an early age she wanted to write powerful heroines and fulfills that dream by writing badass empowered heroines who take charge in their paranormal worlds.

Susan grew up on a thoroughbred horse farm before moving to the big city of Dallas. She considers herself a Texan but is loyal to her home state of Arkansas. A lover of travel, she has visited several countries with many more to go on her list. She particularly loved dowsing at Stonehenge and seeing the Parthenon in Athens. The outdoors is a place where Susan finds inspiration and can often be found in a park, at the lake, or on a road trip. She especially loves the mountains. Furry animals hold a special place in her heart, and dogs tend to seek her out as a friend.

Connect with her at susanperson.com

WANT TO LEARN MORE ABOUT SUSAN PERSON?

Scan the QR code below to see where you find more of Susan's book or see what reader events she is attending.

Also by Susan Person

The Night and Rain Series

Crown of Night and Rain, Book 1

Title To Be Annunced, Book 2

Title To Be Annunced,, Book 3

Crown of Broken Promises, Prequel

Crown of Ruined Oaths, Book 1.5 *(Coming July 2025)*

The Falling From Hell Series

Fallen, Book 1

Reverie, Book 2

Marred, Book 3

The Blood Moon Prophecy

Queen of Sacrifice, Book 1

Queen of Darkness Book 2

Queen of Moons Book 3

A Vampire Ice Age Series

In Blood & Ice, Book 1

Reclamation In Ice, Book 2

Book 3: TBA

Enchanted Rock Immortals World

Fae Undone, The Enchanted Rock Immortals Clan Fae

Fae Redone, The Enchanted Rock Immortals Clan Fae

www.ingramcontent.com/pod-product-compliance
Lightning Source LLC
Chambersburg PA
CBHW031438200726
48289CB00002BA/635